The SEDUCTION of PRETTY LIES

The
SEDUCTION
of
PRETTY LIES

HOLLY RENEE

FOR KATIE CONDIE

Thank you for loving my book babies as much as I do.

Olly belongs to you.

PROLOGUE
OLLY

Two Years Earlier

God, she was so pretty.

I clenched my hand at my side to avoid reaching out and touching her.

She was also too young for me and she was my best friend's little sister, but neither of those things seemed to matter when I was looking at her.

I was always looking at her, but she was looking at him.

Lucas grinned at her from across the table, and a soft blush bloomed across her cheeks. He was one of my best friends too, but I wanted to kill him when he looked at her like that. My stomach hardened as I watched them. I knew I didn't have the right. She wasn't mine, but for some reason, she felt like it.

She had felt like it for far longer than I liked to admit.

"What are you up to today, Frankie?"

She pulled her attention away from Lucas long enough

to look over at me. "Not a whole lot. I thought I might go for a swim before the party tonight. You're going, right?"

"Yeah." I nodded. "I'll be there."

"Good." She smiled at me as she leaned against her hand. "What about you, Lucas? Are you going to be there?"

I clenched my teeth as I waited for his response. He always treated Frankie as if she wasn't important. He treated her like she wasn't the most important person in the room even though she looked at him like he was the most crucial thing in her life.

"Of course." He rubbed his hands together as he talked, but he was barely looking at her. "I need to get fucked up or laid tonight."

Frankie's shoulder slumped the smallest bit, and she looked away before either of us could see her face.

A face I knew she was attempting to school to hide her hurt.

"Real classy, Lucas." I rolled my eyes because even though I had been friends with Lucas for what felt like forever, I still didn't see what Frankie saw in him. I was beginning to wonder why I was friends with him at all. "Come on, Frankie. Let's go hit the beach before the party."

"Okay." She nodded and stood from her seat. "Let me grab my suit."

As soon as she left the kitchen, Lucas leaned back in his chair and chuckled.

"What the fuck is wrong with you?" I glared at him.

"What's wrong with you?" He laughed harder. "You look like a lovesick puppy over Beck's little sister when you can get any pussy you want in the entire school. Don't let a piece of ass make you look so pathetic."

"Don't fucking talk about her like that." My pulse was

racing as I clenched my fists at my sides. "You have no idea..."

"What are you assholes talking about?" Beck interrupted us as he walked into the kitchen and grabbed an apple off the island.

"Trying to get Olly laid." Lucas smirked, and my fingers tingled with the urge to knock it off his face.

"It's about damn time." Beck wrapped an arm over my shoulder and laughed. "You've been a little tense."

"Fuck you both." I shrugged Beck off me just as Frankie came back around the corner. She was wearing a simple black bikini, but I couldn't look away.

"Hey, you ready?" She held a towel against her stomach, and I watched as her eyes flashed over to Lucas before looking back at me.

"Yeah. Let's go." I opened the back door and waited for her to walk through. This was Frankie's house, but I felt like I knew it as well as my own. I practically lived here most days.

Frankie walked in front of me, and I stared at the soft slope of her back as she pushed through the back gate and out onto the sand.

"Is it just me, or does Lucas seem like he's in a bad mood?" She looked back over her shoulder at me. She pushed her hair out of her face before looking back down at the sand.

"He's just being a dick." I pulled my t-shirt over my head and tossed it down. "Don't let him bother you."

"I'm not." She looked back to the house, and we both knew she was lying. She tossed her towel down on top of my shirt, then followed me into the ocean. "I just don't like when any of you are upset. Speaking of, did your dad show up to your game last night? I didn't see him."

"No." I laughed it off because Frankie and I both knew that wasn't something I wanted to talk about. "He had to work."

He always had to work. Him and my mom both.

But don't change the subject on me. We both know you like Lucas, and we also both know that he's not the guy for you.

I was. I didn't dare say that out loud. I shouldn't have been thinking about my best friend's little sister at all, but the idea of her doing anything with Lucas made me feel irrational.

"You don't know that." Her jaw clenched as she turned toward me. "What's going on with you two, anyway? You're supposed to be friends."

"We are friends." I ran my wet hand through my hair and pushed the thick strands back out of my face. "And I know him better than you do. Trust me when I tell you that you deserve better."

I knew what kind of asshole it made me to be talking about my friend like this, but I saw the way he treated girls. They were nothing more than easy fucks or a leg up in some way.

He was just like his stepdad, and there was no way in hell I was going to allow him to use Frankie in either of those ways.

I knew Beck wouldn't either. Hell, Beck would probably kill me if he had any fucking clue of the inappropriate thoughts I had about his sister, but Beck didn't see Lucas the way I did.

He didn't see the way he acted around Frankie because he never did it in front of him.

But I saw everything when it came to her.

"I think you think too highly of me, Olly." She sank into the water, and I watched as the water rolled over her shoulders.

"No. You just think too little." Shit. That came out wrong. She chuckled and splashed some water at my chest. "You know what I mean. You don't see you the way I see you."

Her head cocked to the side as she studied me, and I shifted on my feet. She was within arm's reach of me, and I could have easily pulled her toward me and tasted her lips that had been haunting me.

"And how do you see me, Olly?" She swam closer to me, and the gentle waves of the ocean felt like they were suddenly beating against me.

"I..." *God, were her eyes always that dark?* "I..."

"Frankie! Mom wants you!" The sound of Beck's voice made me jerk back away from her even though there was still plenty of distance.

Frankie blinked, and I could have sworn she was looking at me differently than she was only moments before. This girl was fucking with my head.

Maybe Lucas was right. Maybe I did need to get laid.

But when I closed my eyes and held my cock in my hand, she was all I could think about. I had never been so screwed up over a girl, but why did it have to be her?

Lucas was right when he said I could have had almost any girl in school that I wanted, but I couldn't seem to force myself to want any of them. And trust me, I desperately wanted to.

I would have given anything to stop wanting Frankie the way I did.

"I'm coming!" Frankie yelled back to Beck, but she was still looking at me.

I felt like I could barely breathe as she watched me, her dark brown eyes flicking back and forth between mine, and I had no idea what she was searching for.

But I would have given it to her.

If only she was looking at me like she looked at him. I would have given her anything.

"You should head in. I'm going to swim for a bit and clear my head."

"Okay." She nodded and hesitated only for a second before she headed out of the water. "We'll talk about this later, though?"

"Of course." I smiled at her and rubbed the back of my neck.

But I never should have let her go.

CHAPTER 1
FRANKIE

Two Years Later

Summer was just about to begin, but the water was still freezing. It nipped at my ankles as I slowly pushed through the sand and forced myself into the ocean.

"Come on." Olly reached his hand out for me and grinned. He had already dived headfirst into the water, and his wet, brown hair was pushed back out of his eyes.

Did he have to be so damn handsome?

"It's cold." I wrapped my arms around my chest, and his gaze fell there as if that one simple movement was a magnet. Goose bumps broke out across my skin, and I told myself that it was simply from the water and had nothing to do with the way my friend was looking at me.

"Don't be a chicken, Frankie. It's not that bad." He stepped closer to me, and there was a spark of mischief in his eyes that made my heart race.

"No!" I squealed just as his arms wrapped around my middle, and he lifted me onto his shoulder.

I didn't want to be thrown in that damn cold water, but God, it felt so good to have his arms wrapped around me. To feel his skin pressed against mine.

It made me feel like I was suddenly on fire, and only he could stifle the flames that felt like they were devouring me.

How someone could have so much power over me without even trying was pathetic.

It was more than pathetic honestly, but I also couldn't bring myself to care. Every moment that I got to spend with him fueled me. It made me want him more even though I knew that was the last freaking thing that should happen between us.

If Beck hadn't wanted me to date one of his friends before, Lucas had obliterated that option with everything he did to me. To them.

Pain sliced through my chest at the thought, and my body tensed against Olly. He noticed it immediately, and I could feel the tension in his own frame.

Of course, he noticed.

He noticed everything, and he could always see through me so easily.

He read my body so effortlessly, and most of the time, I felt like he could read my mind too. That was what worried me the most because he had to know. He had to realize exactly what I felt for him.

Because even though I tried to hide it, I didn't stand a chance.

I felt like everything about me was screaming how badly I wanted him, how desperately I needed him. Olly knew. He had to. Even if he tried to act like he didn't. Even if he tried to pretend like we were the happiest little friends who had nothing else going on between us.

He was a fool, and so was Beck if he didn't see it.

We all were.

Olly slowly lowered me down against his body into the water instead of throwing me, and I was hyperaware of every inch of my skin that touched his.

His brows were drawn together, and I couldn't miss the way he clenched his jaw as he looked me over.

For once, I just wanted to be any other girl that he wanted. I hated that I had become something more yet less all at the same time. That I had become the girl they all felt like they had to protect.

The girl that was broken.

I didn't want Olly to protect me. I wanted... I don't know. More.

"You okay?" His voice was so low that I knew I was the only one to hear his question, and I knew he was trying to spare me from the others.

"Of course." I laughed and tried to deflect his concern. I splashed water at his chest and shivered. "There was just no way I was letting you throw me in this water."

"It's just..." His gaze ran down my body, and I knew that he was overthinking the way I tensed above him. He over-thought everything.

"I'm fine, Olly." I gave him a look that begged him to drop it before running my hand over the water.

He didn't believe me. I could see the doubt staring back at me, and I hated it. I hated how breakable he thought I was. I knew everything that happened with Lucas had affected him as much as it did Beck. They felt betrayed and defensive, but I wished that I could just take it all away.

I never wanted to think about it again.

I never wanted to remember how idiotic I had been with

Lucas. I didn't want to still feel his hands on my skin when I had a night of restless sleep that startled me awake.

But more than any of that, I didn't want Olly to look at me like he was looking at me now. Like I was damaged.

"This water is cold as hell." I startled and looked over at Carson just as he pushed past me into the ocean. His arms wrapped around his chest, and he was tiptoeing through the water with a wince. "I'm pretty sure my dick just shriveled away."

I chuckled and let my shoulders relax as I turned toward him. "Poor Allie."

"He'll come back out to play for her." Carson winked at me, and I rolled my eyes. Allie caught up to him in the water and smacked his arm.

"You are so inappropriate."

"Yeah, but you love that about me." He wrapped his arms around her and pulled her farther into the water with him.

I followed them, step after step, taking me farther away from Olly, but his fingers trailed against mine under the water. My chest fluttered, and I looked back at him over my shoulder. His attention was on Carson, and if I still hadn't felt his skin on mine, I would have thought I was imagining the entire thing.

"Did you get that package from the university yesterday?" Olly asked, and my back straightened.

"Yeah." Carson tucked Allie tighter against his chest, and she smiled up at him as she ran her fingers over his skin. Jealousy bloomed in my chest at what they had. I was so happy for both of them, but I was also envious. "Thank fuck they gave us a place together. I was ready to go kick down Coach's door if they didn't."

"Because he's going to care what the new freshman on

the team want?" Olly cocked an eyebrow and his fingers slipped from mine.

"He will if he wants us to play worth a damn. I'm high maintenance. I need you near or I won't do well." Carson batted his eyelashes at Olly, and I snorted out a laugh even as my chest was tightening.

Olly was leaving.

"Plus, I won't have to put a sock on the door whenever Allie comes to visit. You'll just know."

"Oh my God." Allie slapped him again before pressing her forehead against his chest. "I swear, you're so damn embarrassing."

"If you're embarrassed now, maybe we do need a sock." Carson chuckled and wagged his eyebrows.

"I'll just find someone to stay with whenever Allie visits." Olly shuddered with a laugh. "I don't need to hear all that."

"Oh! Like a girl?" Carson teased him, but it felt like a dagger to my chest.

I swallowed and ran my fingers through the water. Allie looked over at me, and I knew that she could see right through me. It didn't matter how much I had practiced schooling my features when it came to Olly. The pain of imagining him with someone else was a punch to the gut that I couldn't hide.

No amount of preparing myself for the inevitable helped. Not in the slightest. I wasn't foolish enough to think that Olly wasn't going to go to college and be with other girls. I knew that he was probably sleeping with girls here.

Of course, he was.

But he didn't rub it in my face here. I saw the way girls looked at him, the amount of attention he got, and I didn't blame them. Olly was handsome, and he was also different.

He was so damn different than every other guy I had ever met.

He didn't see me because of my money, my family, or my looks. Olly saw the real me that I wasn't sure anyone else ever had. He saw me when no one else seemed to be looking.

He didn't need his dark brown hair, the dark stubble that covered his face, or the golden tan that coated his skin. He would be the most attractive guy in Clermont Bay without all that.

He always had been.

And I was sure that the girls in California would notice it as easily as I did.

"I'd rather sleep in the locker room than listen to you two," Olly joked, and I wondered if he did so for my benefit.

"Where are Beck and Josie?" I shielded my eyes from the blinding sun and looked back up at my house.

"Beck was helping Josie get into her bikini when we came down, so I doubt we'll see them anytime soon." Allie giggled and wrapped her arms around Carson's neck.

Carson nuzzled against her and Allie giggled harder. I felt like I was eavesdropping on a private moment between them, so I quickly turned away and looked back to Olly.

"I think I'm going to get out." I nodded my head toward the beach, but he grabbed my hand under the water again and tugged me toward him.

"I'm going to be gone to California soon. Don't you want to spend all the time with me you can before I leave?" He gave me a teasing smile, and his fingers toyed with mine.

"Please don't remind me." I pouted playfully even though I really didn't want to be reminded of it, and he pushed my hair over my shoulder. He lingered there, his gaze boring into me, and my mouth fell open as I tried to breathe.

His gaze dropped there, watching my mouth for far too long to ever be considered innocent. It lowered further, dragging over every inch of me before he pulled me farther out into the water with my hand in his.

I didn't fight him. I could barely think with the way he was looking at me, and I followed him into the water without another thought about the cold. My breasts sank into the water before it lapped against my collarbones. We were far enough from Allie and Carson now that I could barely hear their murmurs.

"I hate that look on your face." He lifted his free hand and ran it along my jaw. I shivered under his touch, and I felt like I was falling into him. "You can come to visit me all the time with Allie." He was searching my face, but I had no damn clue what he was looking for. Whatever it was, I would gladly give it to him. I would hand over any part of me that he wanted.

"And sleep in the locker room?" I managed to joke, and he laughed softly against me. He was so close that I could feel the slight rumble of his chest against mine.

"I'll get a really good surround sound system to drown them out." His eyes sparkled with mischief. "Then we can just hide out in my room."

It was right on the tip of my tongue to ask him what he'd do with his girlfriend when I came to visit, but I bit it back. Olly wasn't even mine, but I still sounded like a jealous girlfriend who wasn't willing to let him go. Not even a little bit.

"What is it?" He cocked his head to the side as he studied me, and his fingers locked with mine under the water. Always in the shadows.

"Nothing." I shook my head, and I wished with everything inside me that it were the truth.

"Don't lie to me. You know I can read you better than that." His fingers tightened along with my chest.

I wanted to scream. I wanted to do anything that would stop me from feeling like I was going crazy. "Honestly, it's nothing."

"Frankie."

"Olly," I said his name with the same exasperated exhale in which he said mine.

"You know you'll always be my girl even when I'm there." His words sounded so sincere, but I knew that they meant something different to him than they did to me. I was his girl like I was Beck's or Carson's. I was his friend, his little sister, the furthest thing from what I wanted to be.

"Yeah." I nodded and attempted to pull away from him, but he refused to loosen his grip on me.

"What's wrong then?" His gaze fell from my eyes to my mouth, and everything inside me screamed at me to close the gap between us. I desperately wanted to kiss him to see if his lips tasted exactly like I imagined they would.

I wondered if they would be as gentle as his hands were against mine or if he would lose control at the first taste of me. Would the calm, controlled Olly cease to exist or would he remain that disciplined as I fell apart around him?

"I don't think your girlfriends will really like me coming to California to visit you." I was honest with him for the first time in what felt like forever. We never talked about this. We never ventured further than the secret touches and longing moments that I was starting to think were one-sided.

"I don't have any girlfriends, Frankie."

"But you will." I nodded because I knew that was the truth, and I needed the reminder more than he did.

"And you will have guys dying for your attention." A

deep line formed between his brows as they scrunched together, and I could have sworn that look was one of jealousy.

"Oh, yes." I pulled my hand from his and leaned back, letting the cold water soak into my hair. "Because I'm such a hot commodity now."

"I see the way they all look at you." He stared down at me for a second before his gaze roamed down my body. It was as if he was physically touching me. Everywhere his gaze went, a trail of electricity followed. "They all want you, Frankie."

"Not all of them." My stomach tightened, and his gaze stopped there. His brow was still scrunched as if he was trying to work something out in his head, and I was dying to reach up and smooth it out.

"All of them. Trust me."

I stood back up, digging my toes into the sand, and watched as he clenched his hands into fists at his sides.

"Even you?" I whispered the question, and for a second, I didn't think he heard me. He was so fucking still that I couldn't breathe, and I wished I could take back what I had asked him.

"You know I can't answer that."

"Why not?" I could feel the rivulets of water running down my body from my hair, and his gaze followed their path.

"It's not fair to either of us." He finally looked at me, really looked at me, and I hated what I saw.

"Because of my brother?" I was as frustrated as I sounded.

"Because of him. Because of..." He trailed off, so I finished the sentence for him so he didn't have to say it.

"Lucas?" I crossed my arms over my chest, but it wasn't

enough. I felt so exposed even saying his name. "What he did has nothing to do with you and me."

But when I thought about it, all I could think about were the things Olly had said to me before. If only I had listened to him. If only I had realized how much better Olly was then, then maybe…

"I know that." He ran his wet hand through his hair, and his jaw clenched. I didn't know if it was frustration or anger, but I didn't deserve either. "That's not what I meant. It's just that he made things harder. Beck would never forgive me."

I knew what he was saying was true, but I still hated it. I wasn't just his best friend's little sister. I was his best friend's little sister who was assaulted by her brother's other best friend. By a guy I had once trusted as much as the rest of them.

As much as I did him.

But his words still cut through me and ripped open wounds I tried not to think about.

"And I'm leaving. This is my last summer before—"

"I know," I interrupted him. My head was starting to throb from my deep, rapid pulse that coursed through me. "Before this is all over."

I planted a fake smile on my face and looked up at him. *Hide it, Frankie. Don't let him see how badly this hurts you.*

"That doesn't mean…" He stepped closer to me, and I wasn't sure if he even realized he was doing it.

"Mean what?" I asked, and I was so damn desperate for his answer.

"That…" He hesitated again, and I wanted to shake him.

"Just say it, Olly. Say what you're really thinking." My heart hammered, and no matter how hard I tried, I couldn't calm it down.

"That I want you any less." His gaze was molten as it met mine. "I can be halfway across the world from you, and I'll still want you more than you'll ever realize."

I tried to swallow down a breath, but it felt impossible.

"Olly," I whispered his name, and it sounded like a plea.

We were so close now that I could feel the heat of his skin. He reached for my hand again, but the moment his skin met mine, I heard my brother's voice behind us.

"How cold is it?" Beck called out, and Olly dropped his hand from mine so quickly you would think I burned him.

"Freezing." Olly laughed as he took a step back from me and ran his fingers down his neck. I wrapped my arms around my chest as I watched him.

Olly stared up at my brother and didn't meet my eyes.

Pain sliced through my chest because I wanted him to pick me. I knew that was selfish. I knew that I shouldn't have wished for something that would eventually hurt someone that I loved, but I did.

Despite what Beck thought or wanted, hell, what anyone thought, I wanted Olly.

I wanted him to choose me and to make this constant buzzing in my head disappear. More than anything, I wanted him to choose me in a way that made me feel like I wasn't their burden.

I was tired of being the girl who didn't have more because of what happened to her. I was exhausted of being the girl who couldn't want to be with someone because I should have been frightened by anything sexual.

I wasn't scared of anything when it came to Olly except for the fact that he may not have wanted me the way I wanted him.

That thought terrified me.

He finally glanced back in my direction, and the way he was looking at me now was so different than only moments before. "This can't happen, Frankie." His hand motioned gently between the two of us. "I'm not good for you. You need to live. Have fun. This is your senior year, and you don't need to spend it stuck with me."

Anger bubbled to the surface, but I tried to push it down. Even though I tried not to be, I was angry with him for a choice he was making for me even though it was the last thing I wanted.

But anger felt so much better than desperation.

CHAPTER 2

OLLY

I pushed through the crowd in search of Frankie. She had barely spoken to me since yesterday, and I wasn't dumb enough to pretend like I didn't know why.

I should have never opened my fucking mouth.

I had made it this long keeping myself in check, and trust me, I had wanted to tell Frankie everything for as long as I could remember. I wanted to whisper every single thing I was thinking about her against her skin while I explored every inch of her perfect body. I was dying to taste her lips, to taste her moans.

I was desperate to just hold her and make her feel like more than anyone had ever made her feel before.

Maybe one day. That thought echoed in my mind on repeat, and I tried to quiet it. I was meant to be the guy Frankie needed and not the guy I wanted to be to her. One day meant someone would get hurt. One day meant that I was going to have to face everything I felt for her, and I didn't know if I dared.

I knew how big of a coward that made me.

Because even though she looked at me like she lost as much sleep over me as I did her, I was fucking terrified that she didn't.

I was frozen by the thought of not being able to breathe while I was simply someone who had been helping her survive through her pain.

It was so much easier to not say anything at all than to face that.

I needed her, and she needed so much more. Everything I felt for her felt chaotic and reckless, and fuck, that felt so dangerous.

Because regardless of what she wanted, we couldn't have any of it.

Beck would never forgive me if I crossed that line with her. He may have before. Before Lucas fucked everything up, but he trusted me. He trusted me and Carson to protect his sister just like he would.

He had trusted Lucas that way once upon a time too, and he fucking broke him when he betrayed him. He changed Beck in a way that I couldn't describe, and I knew there was no going back from that.

But none of that compared to what he did to Frankie.

Every time I thought about it, I wanted to kill him. He was just allowed to walk around, to live, after what he did, and my hands shook with fury every time I saw him.

I was meant to be another one of her protectors, not the guy fantasizing about her like I was an addict and she had become my drug of choice.

But fuck, she was an addiction that I wasn't sure I could break.

But I knew that she was the one capable of breaking me. I had become a safe place for Frankie, a shield against the rest of the world, and more than anything, I feared that safety was where her desire lied. While I was utterly consumed by her, I had become her harbor.

I spotted her standing next to a group of people I knew from school, and she was laughing at something the guy next to her had just said. I watched as she backed away from him less than half a step as he leaned closer to her. He didn't have a clue. There were some things that she always did to protect herself, and they were almost undetectable if you weren't looking.

But I always saw.

"Hey." I stepped up next to her and pressed my hand to the small of her back. Her body sagged against my hand just the tiniest bit as if it recognized the feel of me before she turned in my direction. I could physically feel the tension leaving her body, and I instantly went on alert.

Had someone made her feel uncomfortable or was she just overwhelmed altogether?

"Hi." She barely met my eyes as she spoke, and I knew that I had really fucked things up when she turned back to the guy in front of her and gave him her attention.

I recognized him, but I couldn't remember his damn name. John? Jimmy? Fuck, what was it?

"Hey, man." I nodded to him and tightened my grip on Frankie. My fingers bunched in her shirt, and I knew there was no way she didn't notice. "I'm Olly."

"Of course." He chuckled and looked back and forth between me and my girl. "I'm Jarod."

Jarod. Shit, I knew that.

"Jarod, do you mind if I borrow Frankie for just a second? We really need to talk."

He opened his mouth to answer, but Frankie beat him to

it. "Actually, it'll have to wait." She looked back at me and gave me a look that told me she wasn't fucking around. There was so much fire in her gaze that it almost hid the sadness that was always lingering. "Jarod was just about to show me something."

I tightened my grip on the back of her shirt but smiled. "Okay. I can wait."

I wasn't sure if I would ever stop waiting.

She didn't answer me, and I didn't hang around to see what the hell Jarod was going to show her. Frankie rarely ever talked to guys at a party; most of the time she was by my side if she even came at all, but I knew that this probably had everything to do with what I said yesterday.

I grabbed a beer out of a cooler as I passed by and clenched my hand around the cold glass as I walked away from her and out the back of the house.

I spotted Carson as soon as I walked out the door, and he cocked his head to the side as if he was studying me. I wondered if he had been watching me with her the whole time.

Fuck. I needed to stop being an idiot. If Carson could see through me so easily, then that meant other people could too.

"What's up?" I twisted the top off my beer and brought it to my lips without waiting for anyone's reply. Josie was sitting on Beck's lap and leaning against his chest. Allie was standing behind Carson with her arms wrapped around his stomach.

My chest tightened as I looked over at them all. I was happy for all of them. More than happy, but I wanted that. I wanted to be able to pull Frankie out here and hold her the way they were holding them.

But more than anything, I just wanted to pull her away from that douchebag in there.

I looked back through the door, and my gaze met hers before she quickly looked away. She smiled at something he said, but her arms were crossed over her chest. She didn't look at him for long. Her eyes bounced around the room and watched those around her. She was always so aware of her surroundings, and my stomach knotted because I hated the thought that she always felt she needed to.

Jarod was smiling at her like he was the luckiest guy alive, and I knew he wasn't picking up on one bit of her unease.

And even though I wanted to hate him, I knew that wasn't his fault.

Frankie was gorgeous. Her dark brown hair and tanned skin were a lethal combination, and she had become so good at hiding her mistrust.

Frankie was capable of making you forget anything other than her even existed.

She looked back up at him, and I knew if he wasn't distracted by her perfect pink lips, then he was looking into her eyes. They were so dark brown that they were almost black, and she showed so much emotion with them. I had never met anyone who could be so vulnerable with just a single look.

But she was.

With me, she never seemed to hide it.

It was something that I both loved and hated about her.

I almost always knew how she felt, but that meant I could never hide from it either. Whenever I was doing my fucking best to bury everything I was feeling for her, she simply looked up at me and all the work I had done was unraveled.

"Where's Frankie?" Beck looked up at me like I should have the answer. "She came with us, but I haven't seen her in a while." He stood like he was going to go look for her, but I quickly nodded into the house.

"In there." I didn't pretend like I had taken my eyes off her for a single second and pointed to where she stood with the neck of my beer bottle. "She told me that Jarod was showing her something."

"What the fuck is he showing her?" Beck growled, and I wished that he would storm in there and pull her away from him. But that didn't happen.

"Leave her alone." Josie gripped his jaw in her hand and turned his gaze back to meet hers. "You all are going to have to let the girl live a little whether you like it or not."

"Not with Jarod," Beck grumbled, and Carson snorted out a laugh. But I had to agree with Beck on this one.

"Yes. With Jarod." Josie sounded so irritated. "Or Tom or Billy or Enrique. It's not up to the three of you who Frankie decides to date, and pretty soon, the three of you will have graduated and she's going to get all the attention they've been too scared to give her."

She was right, but she was also wrong. It wasn't up to us who Frankie decided to date, but I would be damned if I let my girl fall for some fucking douchebag. She had already been hurt so much in her lifetime, and she didn't deserve any more. Not from them and not from me.

Frankie deserved to experience life and have fun. She deserved so much more than anyone in this town had ever given her, and I hated the idea of her getting stuck.

Beck said something back to Josie, but I was too busy

watching Frankie to hear what he said. Jarod moved closer to her and pressed his hand against the small of her back, my spot, and his hand laid flat against her skin where her shirt had lifted. I watched her tense under his touch, but she didn't move away. I downed the rest of my beer as my blood raced through my veins.

I think Beck was asking a question, maybe to me, maybe to someone else, but I didn't care either way. I tossed my beer bottle in the trash before pushing back through the door and making my way toward Frankie.

She smiled up at Jarod, but her jaw was clenched tightly. Why the fuck was she letting him touch her?

Her gaze lifted to me, and I saw the small flash of relief in her eyes even though she tried to hide it.

"Frankie, I need to talk to you for a sec." I crossed my arms and stared down at where Jarod was still touching her. I was seconds away from ripping his damn arm off.

"Seriously, Olly?" She sighed my name, and Jarod slowly pulled his hand off her back.

I finally looked back up at her and the relief I had seen a few moments before was gone and had been replaced with irritation. Good. I was beyond irritated myself.

"You don't have to talk to me if you don't want. I can let Beck come in here like he wanted to." I hiked my thumb over my shoulder to where I knew her brother was still sitting. No doubt they were all watching us, but I couldn't bring myself to care.

"Fine." She practically growled and pulled away from him. "Jarod, excuse me. I'll be right back."

She stomped away a few steps without waiting for me, and I took a step closer to Jarod. For all I knew, he was a great guy. Hell, he could probably treat Frankie far better than I would ever get the opportunity to, but I wasn't willing to give him the opportunity either. Seeing his hand on her felt like he was violating something that didn't belong to him.

He wasn't right for her.

"She won't be back."

His gaze flew up to mine, and I was glad I had his attention.

"I thought Frankie was single."

"She's not." I shook my head as I clenched my jaw, and even though it was a lie, it felt like the most honest thing I had said all day. "So I suggest you stay away from her."

I walked past him in search of Frankie, and I didn't have to go far. She was still only a few steps away, and she was staring at me like she wanted to murder me. I knew that she had heard everything I just said, but I couldn't bring myself to be sorry. I meant it whether it was right or wrong.

She stormed away from me as I headed toward her, and I couldn't blame her for being pissed. But she had to know there was no way in hell I could just sit back and watch her with someone else. It wasn't fair. I was more than aware of that.

Hurting her was the last thing I wanted to do, but I didn't know how to love her and not hurt her in some way.

I didn't know how to be this guy who had become her protector while also not making her feel stuck.

Frankie had watched me with other girls, and there had been plenty. But I hadn't touched anyone else in over two years. Two fucking excruciating years.

I tried. Trust me, I wished that I could just fuck someone else and get Frankie out of my system, but it didn't work that way. She was embedded so deeply in me that I wasn't sure I would ever be able to get her out. I wasn't sure that I wanted to.

I snatched her hand in mine as I caught up to her, but she jerked it away as she kept walking.

"Frankie," I sighed, and she only stormed faster down the hallway. "Hold on. Just fucking talk to me."

She stopped in her tracks, my chest almost hitting her back, and she spun toward me. There was so much fire in her eyes as she stared up at me. "Why the hell would you tell him that I'm with someone." She held out her hands to her sides as her voice rose. "I think it's clear as fucking day that I'm not."

A few people turned in our direction before I gripped her wrist in my hand and tugged her farther down the hall. The first door I tried to open was locked, and I cursed under my breath as I went for the next. Thankfully, this one opened, and I pulled Frankie inside behind me before closing the door.

"Will you calm down?"

"No!" She jerked her wrist out of my touch and pressed her trembling hands into her hips. "I will not calm down, Olly. I don't know who the hell you think you are, but you do not get to decide who I do or don't date."

I took a step toward her, and she held up her hand to keep me at bay. "You don't get to decide who I kiss or touch or fuck." Her voice shook on the last word, and I pressed my chest against her hand and closed the space between us whether she wanted me to or not.

"You know that's a lie." I stared down at her and moved some of her dark brown hair out of her face. The room was dark with only the light of the moon filtering in through the window, but I could still see her. I had always been able to see her.

"It's not." She shook her head before I pressed my hand against her neck and stopped her movement with my thumb.

I felt the way her breath trembled in and out of her throat under my touch. She was so fucking beautiful. Far too beautiful for anyone at this damn party, but I couldn't stop myself from touching her. I lifted my thumb and ran it across her full bottom lip, and it was so damn soft. Softer than I had ever imagined.

"You and I both know it is." I pushed even closer to her, and her hand flattened between us. "I'd kill that asshole before I let him have what is mine."

She let out a whimper that almost dropped me to my knees. "I'm not yours, Olly." Her words were no longer sure, the bite from earlier had all but disappeared.

"You are." I leaned in and ran my nose along her jaw. "It doesn't matter what anyone else says or thinks. You are mine."

She shoved against my chest, but I didn't budge. I couldn't. Not when I was so fucking close to her, and I could smell the slightest hint of coconut on her skin.

"Olly," she whispered my name, and it sounded like the sweetest plea on her lips.

I couldn't control myself. After all this time, I couldn't wait another second. I lifted her chin until she was forced to look back up at me, and I closed the gap between us. Without even truly deciding to, my mouth met hers in a rush. She moaned into my mouth as she met my lips with just as much force.

I ran my tongue over the seam of her lips, and she

opened without hesitation. My body felt like it was on fire as her tongue ran over mine. I kissed her like I may never get the chance again, and I could feel myself losing bits of who I was in her with every passing second.

Frankie pulled her arms from between us before she wrapped them around my shoulders. Her fingers tangled in the back of my hair, and there was the slightest sting of pain as she forced me impossibly closer to her.

What started as a rushed, frantic kiss became slower and more purposeful. Frankie wrapped one of her legs around my waist, and I pressed firmly against her. She didn't stop me. Instead, she met my hips with her own, and when I gripped her ass in my hands she lifted her other leg and wrapped fully around me. She began to move, her hips as slow as her tongue, and I thought I was going to die from the torture.

I felt so impatient for her touch. I wanted to feel her everywhere. I wanted to sink into the wildest parts of her.

I ran my tongue and lips over her jaw and down her neck, and she tasted exactly as she smelled. Frankie was a mixture of sunshine and the ocean. She was like that exact spot where they met, where everything seemed magical, elusive, and so far out of reach.

"Olly, please," she whispered my name, and it sounded like a fucking prayer.

She was still rolling her hips against mine, and I knew she could feel how hard I was for her. I could feel her too. Every inch of her moved against me in a way that should have had me questioning her innocence, and I moved a hand from her ass to slowly creep up her body. Her stomach tremored beneath my touch as my fingers ran over her skin, but there wasn't an ounce of fear in her eyes. It was one hundred percent raw anticipation that was waiting for me.

Frankie wanted me. I was absolutely certain that she wanted me physically, and God, I wanted her too. I had wanted her for so long that this moment felt like a recurrent dream that had haunted me night after night.

Every time I closed my eyes, she was the only thing I could picture.

She was both hedonic and torturous at the same time.

And here she was beneath my touch and still, she felt so far out of reach. I cupped her small breast in my hand, and I watched as I slowly dragged my thumb over her nipple. She was still fully clothed, but the fabric did little to hide what lay beneath. She moaned loudly, and for the first time since we had walked in the room, my gaze flew to the door behind her that anyone could easily walk in through.

What the fuck were we doing?

I kissed her again because there was no way I could stop. I drank in the taste of her, the feel of her, and she held me to her as she intensified her movements against me as I bit down on her bottom lip before soothing the pain with my tongue. Frankie's hips surged forward as if she couldn't control the movement, and I could only imagine how wet her pussy was.

I was dying to know. I was dying to rip her pants down her legs and bury my face in her sweet pussy until everyone in this entire fucking place knew who she belonged to.

I gripped her ass in my hands again and took a steadying breath against her mouth. There is no way that she would stop this. She didn't give a shit about what her brother or anyone else thought, but I did. Beck was not just my best friend. He was my brother, and he would hate me for this.

This wasn't a normal brother's best friend situation. He entrusted me to protect her, to be the opposite of Lucas, and I was betraying his trust with every second that passed.

But more importantly, I felt like I was betraying hers. She felt safe with me, and I didn't want to take advantage of that feeling.

"Frankie," I breathed her name against her lips and tried to force her hips from mine. She tightened her legs against my waist and her arms on my shoulders.

"Don't." She shook her head, and there was a flash of regret in her eyes. She knew what I was doing. She knew that I couldn't go any further than this. That I had already done too much.

"We can't do this." I searched her eyes before she looked away from me and dropped her feet back to the ground. I would've done anything to take that look away from her at that moment, but I didn't know how. I didn't know how to navigate this without hurting her or fucking up my friendship with Beck.

After everything Frankie had been through, here I was being a damn idiot at another party, taking advantage of her body. She deserved better than this. She deserved more than I would ever be able to give her. But fuck, I wanted to be the one to figure it out.

"It's fine." Frankie straightened her shirt and tucked her hair behind her ears. She still refused to look at me, and her chest still heaved in her attempts to catch her breath.

"Frankie." I reached out for her, but she slipped away from my touch before I could touch her.

"No." She shook her head, and I could see the hurt all over her face. Her chin trembled as her next words hit me. "You don't get to do that. You don't get to pretend like you want me when no one else is around. I'm so tired of being in the shadows."

She was right, and I had no idea what I should say to make any of this up to her. I was desperate to take back what I had done even though I knew I would truly never regret a single second of it. Even if I knew that I should.

She didn't give me the opportunity to do anything. She opened the door before I could string together a few words to tell her how I was feeling, and she stopped dead in her tracks when she saw Beck standing on the other side of the door.

"There you are." He grabbed her hand in his and pulled her toward him, and it took him a few seconds before he finally noticed me behind her. "What the fuck were you two doing?" He narrowed his eyes as he looked back and forth between us.

My heart hammered in my chest because a part of me wanted to just tell him the truth. I wanted to tell him that I had been in love with his sister for a long time, that the things we had done behind that door were something neither one of us could control, but I knew he wouldn't understand that. Beck was my best friend, but he was also irrational and hotheaded, and rightfully so. He was overprotective of Frankie, we all were, but he had reason to be. I couldn't be angry at him for it.

He felt like he failed to protect her once, and he refused to do so again.

"What does it matter?" Frankie huffed and crossed her arms. "What I do with anyone isn't up to you all."

"Frankie," Beck said her name with an exasperated tone. This is a conversation, or better yet, argument, that they had at least a hundred times before.

"What if I told you that I just fucked Olly in that room?" Beck stiffened at her question, and my gaze snapped to her. "What the hell would you do about it if that were the case?"

Beck looked back and forth between me and Frankie, and I couldn't fucking breathe. Because even though we did cross the line in that room, it wasn't what she was saying, and I knew she was just trying to get a rise out of her brother. More than that, she was trying to get a rise out of me.

"I'd kill him." Beck didn't hesitate with his answer, and even though I already knew it, my stomach dropped at his confession.

"Whatever." Frankie rolled her eyes and laughed at her brother. "He's your best friend."

"You're right." He nodded and his gaze landed on me. So much passed between us with that one look than he would ever say out loud. "Which means I trust him more than anyone else. He would never betray me like that."

"Being with me is not a betrayal," Frankie practically screamed, and I stepped forward before this went any further.

"For me, it is." Beck looked back at his sister.

"I was just telling her to stay away from Jarod." The lie fell smoothly from my lips, and my chest fucking ached at how easy it was. "I didn't want to see the poor guy get his ass kicked tonight."

Beck grinned, and I knew he was probably picturing it. "Yeah. He's an asshole, Frankie."

"I hate you."

I thought Frankie was talking to her brother, but when I looked up at her, her gaze was directly on me.

CHAPTER 3
FRANKIE

I couldn't look away from Olly long enough to even see my brother. How he could just stand there like nothing had just happened between us was beyond me. I felt like I was going to explode, like every part of me was shaking with the need to touch him, to kiss him, or to slap him across the face.

Olly wanted me as much as I wanted him, but while I made a conscious decision to want him, his want had been nothing more than a slip of his better judgment.

He regretted everything we had just done even though it had been the best kiss of my life. I knew how sad that was. I knew that Olly was far more experienced than I was, and this was probably just another kiss from any other girl to him. But it meant something to me.

It meant more.

"You'll get over it." Beck laughed because he thought I was talking to him, but I wasn't. I had meant what I said when I told Olly I hated him. At that moment, I did hate him for choosing Beck over me, for letting his friendship with my brother dictate how far we took things, but at the same time, I knew that I could never hate him.

Not really.

"I'm going back out to the party." I pointed down the hall where the loud music was still playing. "And I'm going to find a guy to kiss who doesn't look at me like I'm the biggest mistake of his life." I stared straight at Olly with a heaviness in my chest that I couldn't shake, and I didn't care what Beck thought about what I just said.

"Frankie." Olly looked frantic as he searched my eyes, and I watched his hand unclench at his side to reach out for me. But I refused to let him touch me again. I was too damn angry.

I walked past him before he was able to get to me, and I didn't stop when I heard him or Beck call out my name. I kept pushing through the party, moving past the crowd of people. I spotted Jarod still in the kitchen, but when my gaze met his, he quickly looked away. That was fucking fine with me. I wasn't really interested in him anyway, and no guy that could be so easily intimidated by Olly was worth the effort.

It was better to figure that out early. Even if I had only been talking to him because I desperately wanted to get a reaction out of Olly.

I pushed through the kitchen and made my way out to the back porch. I was met by Josie and Allie staring at me with concerned looks on their faces as soon as the warm air kissed my skin. Allie moved out of Carson's touch, and they both came straight for me before I could say a word.

"Do you want to head home?" Josie asked as soon as she reached me, and I knew that she would leave my asshole brother here and take me home if that was what I wanted. But it wasn't.

I didn't want to go home and wallow in my own fucking pity. I had done that far too much, and I promised myself I wouldn't do it again. Not over some boy.

Even if it was him.

"No." I shook my head. "Let's do something fun."

"What do you want to do?" Allie smiled at me, but there was so much hesitation in that one look. "We're at a party."

I shook my head as a thought about what I wanted, but it wasn't something that the three of us could discuss right now. "I want to get a drink."

They looked at each other with a look of concern, and I knew they thought it was a bad idea. But I didn't care. Everything I did lately seemed like a bad idea.

And I never drank. Not anymore. Not since everything happened with Lucas, but right now, I felt powerless. I felt like every small decision in my life was being made by someone else, and I hated it.

I just wanted to do whatever I wanted. Whether it was smart or not, didn't matter.

I couldn't have Olly because of Lucas and Beck, and the stupid fucking notion that I was somehow everyone else's responsibility. I didn't want to be their burden.

I had become their obligation, and my chest ached at the thought of them seeing me like that.

And I was so tired of making decisions based on what happened in the past. I didn't want to make choices out of fear.

"Okay." Josie nodded. "How about we all get one drink?"

"That's a start." I shrugged as I drew in a deep breath then released it, and she laughed as we made our way over to the keg. I didn't recognize the guy pouring beers, but I didn't give him much thought either. I was too busy chewing on my thumbnail and watching the back door as Olly and Beck pushed through it.

Olly's gaze met mine as soon as he stepped through the threshold, and I jerked my gaze back to the keg.

I knew that I didn't stand a chance in hiding how much he affected me, but I refused to fall at his feet and beg him to give me more than he was willing to give. If he wanted to be just friends, then fine. I could do that.

I would force myself to forget about what it had just felt like to have his mouth and hands on me. I would bury the feeling of being at home in his touch in the very back of my mind.

But I couldn't force myself to unlove him, and I honestly didn't want to.

"Thank you." I took the beer from the guy at the keg, and he smiled up at me with the softest smile.

"Of course, beautiful."

I tightened my hand around my cup and tried to swallow past the heaviness in my throat as I smiled back at him. I should have felt something at hearing him call me beautiful, but I didn't feel anything. Not when I took in his handsome smile or the way he was looking at me like he would have given the world to take me into that room Olly had just forced me out of.

I searched his face and took in his unruly blond hair, but the only thought that crossed my mind was that he wasn't Olly.

I turned away from him and followed Allie back to where the boys were standing. Olly was still watching me. I didn't need to look up at him to know that. I lifted the beer to my mouth and didn't stop when the cold alcohol tasted so bitter on my tongue. I drank more than I knew I should, but deep down, I knew that none of them would let anything happen to me.

Not again.

"Whoa, Frankie." Beck looked concerned as he looked back and forth between me and my drink, but I didn't care. Not tonight.

I didn't reply to his comment. Instead, I swirled the beer in my cup before bringing it back to my mouth and finishing the cup. When I looked up at my friends, all I could see was concern staring back at me from all of them.

From everyone except Olly because I didn't dare look at him.

"I'm going to get another." I shook my empty cup in my hand and pressed my lips together.

"I think you've had enough." Beck's voice was firm, but it was muddled by Olly's. "I'll go with you."

"Nope." I pointed back and forth between both of them and let out a laugh that didn't have an ounce of humor. "I don't need babysitters tonight. You two go find someone else to ruin their night."

I turned away from them before either of them could answer, and headed back to the keg. My stomach tightened as I walked away from them, but I begged it to stop. I just didn't want to feel any of these damn feelings for just a little while.

"That was quick." Keg guy smiled at me before taking the cup from my hand. He was teasing, but he wasn't repri-manding me, and it felt nice.

I shook out my arms and tried to release some of the tension that was trapped inside of me. "I needed a drink."

"Boyfriend problems?" He cocked his head to the side,

and his blond hair flopped into his forehead a little. He was cute. Cuter than I had originally given him credit for.

"More like asshole problems."

He chuckled at my answer and started refilling my cup.

"What about you?" I looked around him. He was basically out here all by himself except for the people who were stopping by for more alcohol. "How did you get stuck manning the keg?"

"Ah. It's not too bad." He handed me my drink before pushing his hair back out of his face. "All the pretty girls come out here for a drink."

I could feel heat rising in my cheeks, and I wondered if he always wore that easy smile on his face. I didn't even know him, but it felt like it fit him so perfectly.

"So, you've met a lot of pretty girls tonight?"

His smile widened as he chuckled softly, and I had a feeling that this guy was genuine. "None as pretty as you."

"If I hadn't just chugged my beer, I'd call you on that lie, but I'll let it slide." I took another sip of my beer as he ran his hand over his jaw before pushing it out in my direction.

"I'm Harry."

"Frankie." I slid my hand in his and let him shake it. It was just another hand that made me feel nothing from its touch.

"Do you go to Clermont High?" He looked me over as if he was trying to place if he had met me before. "I swear I would know you if you do."

"No." I tucked my hair behind my ear as I felt a bit of tension ease from my stomach. "I go to Prep."

"Ahhh. A Prep girl, huh?"

I looked him over from head to toe and didn't answer his question. "A High boy, huh?"

"That's fair." He chuckled, and I genuinely liked the sound.

The fact that he didn't know me was a blessing. It meant he didn't know who my family was, who my brother was, or what had happened to me. Those three things were all most people knew about me these days.

"Can I get a beer?" I heard Olly's voice, but I didn't turn to look at him. My spine straightened as I stared straight ahead at Harry.

"So, Harry, do you have a girlfriend?" I tucked my hand in my back pocket to keep it from shaking.

He looked up from where he was pouring Olly's drink, and there was a spark of surprise in his eyes. "I don't." He looked back and forth between me and Olly quickly.

I nodded my head as I tried to work up my courage. I could feel the anger rolling off Olly next to me, and somehow that only seemed to fuel me on. He didn't have the right to be angry. "I'd love to go out with you sometime if you're interested."

"Absolutely." He over-poured Olly's beer and spilled some over on his hand. He chuckled before shaking the liquid off his hand and holding out Olly's drink for him. He quickly pulled his phone out of his pocket and handed it out to me without another glance in Olly's direction.

"Give me your number, and we can nail down the details."

"Perfect." I glanced up at Olly who was openly glaring at me. Even he couldn't hide the anger that was staring back down at me, and I let my gaze travel down to his flattened lips. "Can you hold this?" I held out my beer in his direction, and it took him a few seconds before he reached out and took it. His fingers trailed over mine, and I knew it wasn't an accident.

Olly didn't know what the hell he wanted from me, but I was sure that he didn't want anyone else to have me. He was unnerving me, trying to distract me from the boy in front of me, but I refused to allow him.

I gripped Harry's phone in both hands as I entered my number with trembling fingers.

"Here you go." I handed it back to him as he grinned.

"I'll text you." He slid his phone into his pocket before his eyes finally went back to Olly. I knew he could feel the tension between us. It would have been impossible for him not to.

"I look forward to it." I grabbed my beer back from Olly's hand and tried not to react when his fingers met mine again. But the small amount of alcohol I had was already starting to mess with my head, and I was physically incapable of not reacting to him when I was completely sober.

I pushed past him before he could say anything to ruin this moment and headed back in the direction of our friends. I could feel Olly on my heels the entire way, and I became so irrationally angry that he wouldn't leave me alone.

"Can I help you with something?" I spun on my heel until I was facing him. He was so damn close to me, and he didn't dare take a step back to give me any room.

"We need to talk." He was so damn calm as he said it, and it just pissed me off more.

"Oh, no!" I pointed my finger into his chest and ground my teeth. "That ship has sailed, buddy."

"Buddy?" His lips tugged up at the edge into a smile and my back straightened. "Am I your buddy now?"

"I wasn't sure if you wouldn't have preferred for me to call you an asshole." I lifted my beer and took a deep swallow. His brows drew together as he watched me.

"You shouldn't be drinking like that."

"And you shouldn't be telling me what to do."

He stared at me like he wanted to argue, but he didn't. He bit his tongue and watched me, and I desperately wished he would just lean down and kiss me in front of everyone. I leaned closer to him, almost subconsciously, and I couldn't read the look on his face.

"Are you going to go out with Harry?"

I smiled at the fact that he knew his name even though I was sure he was going to ruin it for me. "I am. Why? Do you have a problem with that?"

He worked his jaw as he looked away from me, and I knew he was thinking something he wasn't willing to say. "No." He shook his head. "He seems like a good enough guy."

His words shocked me, and my gaze flew up to meet his. "So you're okay with me kissing him?"

When he didn't answer, I stepped even closer and pressed my hand to his chest. "What if we decide to go further? What if I let him touch me?"

"Frankie." My name was a growl on his lips, and I had to press my thighs together to stop the ache that began there.

"Do you think he would touch me like you did in that room?" I nodded my head toward the house and the smell of his cologne surrounded me. I didn't know if it was that or the alcohol that was making me feel so lightheaded. I really hadn't had that much to drink. "Do you think I will go home at the end of the night and replace your name with his when I touch myself?"

"Fuck," he cursed and gripped my bicep in his hand as if he feared I might slip away. There was a bite of pain in his touch, but I didn't want it to stop. "You've had too much to drink."

"Maybe." I shrugged my shoulders. In reality, I had, but these were things I had wanted to say to him for far too long. I just never had the courage. I had always worried too much about what he would think, but I couldn't bring myself to care tonight. "Or maybe Harry just has me really turned on."

"Stop." It was a command.

"Make me." I was so close to him now that I could lean forward and kiss him if I wanted to. He would stop me, of course, but part of me felt like making him. I wanted him to deny me, to break me even further, because maybe then I could forget about him for just a damn second.

"Everyone is watching us," he whispered, and the sound skated down my spine like fingers.

"I don't care."

"Yes. You do." He nodded and pulled me into his body until I was forced to wrap my arms around him. He hugged me against him like he was as desperate to touch me as I was him, and the smallest moan left my lips at the feel of him. "I'm going home. Let me take you back to your house."

"No." I shook my head and pushed against his chest to step back. "I'm staying."

I didn't want to leave. I refused to just let him take me home and pretend like tonight never happened.

He searched my eyes as he pushed his dark hair out of his face, then he let out a heavy sigh. "Then I guess I'm staying too."

CHAPTER 4
OLLY

Frankie had too much to drink.

And even though I probably should have stopped her, I couldn't bring myself to do it.

She was sitting on top of the patio table, and her head was thrown back in laughter. She was so damn beautiful, especially like this, when there wasn't a single worry on her face.

It felt like it had been forever since I had seen her so carefree.

Beck looked up at his sister and chuckled as he watched her. "Are you about ready to go, wild one? Josie has work tomorrow."

"Nope." Her answer was instant and she dramatically popped the P before she reached out and patted her brother on top of his head. "You all can go ahead, though."

"I'm not leaving you here alone." Beck ran his hand over the back of his neck.

"I'm not alone." She glanced around and her eyes connected with mine for what felt like the first time in hours.

"All of my other bodyguards are here, and I'm certain they won't let me get a hair out of place."

"This is true." Carson chuckled and adjusted Allie on his lap. She was so relaxed against him, but her gaze was still on her friend. "I won't let this little one out of my sight."

"Don't call me that," Frankie huffed and crossed her arms, and I smiled at her reaction. She may not have any worries tonight, but she was still as sassy as ever. Maybe even more so.

"Fine." Beck stood and gripped Josie's hand in his. "We'll see you guys tomorrow." Beck looked back and forth between Carson and me as Josie hugged his sister, and we both knew what that one simple look meant.

It was something that I didn't need to forget.

"I love you, Frankie." He tousled her hair, and she rolled her eyes.

"Love you too."

As soon as Beck pushed through the back door, Frankie clapped her hands and grinned. "It's time for another drink."

"How about we slow down?" I took the seat next to her that Beck had just vacated and I instantly felt more at ease being so close to her.

"How about you kiss my ass, Olly? I am not drunk." She smiled sweetly at me.

"Oh shit." Carson laughed and ran his hand over his mouth, and I wanted to kill him. "I think she might have actually had too much to drink."

"I'm having fun." She swung her legs back and forth at the edge of the table and shrugged. "You all are the party poopers."

"Leave her alone." Allie grinned up at her friend. "She's fine."

"Exactly." Frankie turned toward me with a lazy smile and rested her foot on my thigh. "I'm fine."

"Uh-huh." I gripped her ankle in my hand when she tried to turn away from me, and she paused. "Do you want me to get you another drink then?"

"Please." Her legs widened in front of me, and God, what I wouldn't give for us to be anywhere else. For the two of us to be anyone other than who we were.

"I can do that." Carson and Allie were sitting on the opposite side of the table, and I knew if they wanted to, they could see exactly what I was doing. But I still rubbed my thumb along her ankle as I stared up at her. "Is there anything else I can get you?"

"There are several things." She leaned forward so only I could hear her. "But I don't think you want to hear any of those."

My gaze flew up to meet Carson's, but he quickly looked away and tucked his head against Allie as he spoke to her.

"I don't think you have any idea what I want."

Frankie leaned back again and tapped her finger against her chin. "You know what. I don't." Her foot moved the slightest bit higher on my thigh. "And whose fault is that?"

"Mine."

"Yours." She nodded her head in agreement. "Honestly, a lot of things are your fault."

She lifted her other foot and brought it down to rest on my other knee before leaning forward and resting her elbows on her own.

She looked so damn perfect.

"Do tell." I pressed my fingers into her other ankle. "What am I at fault for now?"

"Everything." She sighed before swallowing harshly and

blinking down at me. "You're too damn handsome for your own good."

I leaned forward until my chest pressed against her shins. "Thank you, but I don't see how that makes me guilty of anything."

"It makes you guilty of a lot of things." She held up her hand and started ticking off fingers as she went. "One, I think about you way too often. Two, no other guy will ask me out because you're always around and you're so pretty that you intimidate them."

"What about Harry?" I looked toward the keg, but Harry had disappeared a while ago.

"And three, I can't get off without thinking about your stupid face."

I heard Carson snicker, and I knew it was officially time for us to go. "Okay." I stood, forcing her to lean back slightly, and she looked up at me. "It's time to head home."

"But things are just now getting fun."

"Frankie," I groaned.

"Olly." She repeated my name in the same tone I had just said hers, and I couldn't help but smile. She was too damn cute.

"Come on." I held my hand out to her, and she hesitated before finally slipping her fingers into mine with an eye roll.

"Fine, but just know that I didn't want to leave. You all are the ones who ended this party."

"It's noted." I laughed and looked over at Carson. "I'm taking her home. You need a ride?"

"No." He shook his head and smirked. "I'm good, but be careful with that one."

"I will be."

Frankie said bye to every single person we came across as

we left the party, and I was pretty sure that she didn't know half of their names. I tugged her along as she gave out hugs and air-kisses, and she was a giggling mess by the time we made it to my car.

"I'm coming." She laughed and leaned against the top of the door I had just opened for her. "Don't you ever just want to have a little fun?"

"I had plenty of fun tonight."

She rolled her eyes before sliding into the seat. "You spent more time brooding then having fun. You always do."

I closed the door behind her and moved to the driver's side without answering her. I did have fun tonight. I just couldn't seem to relax when she was around. Especially not with that many people and after everything that had happened.

And definitely not when she had been drinking.

I climbed into my seat and started the engine before looking at her. She had her head turned against the headrest and she was looking at me with the most satisfied look on her face.

"Are you okay?" I lifted my hand and placed it behind her as I backed out of the driveway.

"Never better."

I searched her eyes before putting the car in drive and pulling away from the party.

"You confuse me."

"Welcome to the club." She giggled and shifted in her seat.

"A few minutes ago you were complaining about me ruining your night by making you leave."

"This is true, but even though I have to go home, I now have the memory of you kissing me for the spank bank."

I almost ran off the road at her words. Frankie had never been so bold with the way she was speaking to me. "Jesus Christ, Frankie."

"What?" She shrugged her shoulders and relaxed into my passenger seat. "Would you prefer that I was thinking about someone else or that I get someone else to help me?"

I knew how I should have answered her. I should have told her yes. I should have broken this damn thing between us before we really fucked it up and sent her off to be happy with anyone else. But I couldn't get the damn word to leave my lips. No matter how hard I tried.

"I didn't think so." She chuckled softly, and I looked over just in time to see her run her hand down her neck and over her t-shirt. Her fingers pressed against her breast before it snaked even lower.

"What are you doing?" When she didn't answer me, I glanced back in her direction. "What the hell has gotten into you?"

"Just drive." She sighed. "Nothing has gotten into me. I'm just tired of being the perfect timid girl you all expect me to be." I heard the popping of her jeans button before the loud zipper filled the tight space.

"Fuck, Frankie." I looked over at her before quickly looking back at the road, but I saw her blue fingernails dipping below the edge of her jeans. "Stop."

"I'm not doing anything wrong." She was looking over at me again, and the feel of her, the smell of her, along with the smallest moan that passed her lips was almost my undoing. "Do you ever think of me when you touch yourself, Olly?"

I was so fucking hard against my jeans that it was becoming painful, but this wasn't right. This was crossing a line we couldn't come back from.

"You know I can't answer that."

"I like to imagine that you do." She whimpered as her hands began to move faster beneath her jeans. "I like to pretend that you want me just as badly as I want you. That when your cock is in your hand, you like to imagine that it's mine instead."

I pulled over on the side of the road before I wrecked my damn car and stared at her. She didn't stop her movements, not even for a second, and I knew that she wouldn't stop this unless I forced her to.

And I was no longer capable.

My voice shook as I spoke my next words. "We can't do this."

"We aren't doing anything." She blinked before biting down on her bottom lip. "I'm fingering myself."

"Fuck." Her hand moved beneath the fabric of her jeans, and I could practically imagine exactly what those fingers looked like sliding through her pussy. "Are you wet?"

She whimpered and brought her other hand up to knead her breast. "I'm so fucking wet, Olly."

I pressed my head back against my headrest and tried to control myself as I watched her. I had never seen her look more beautiful than she did right now, and every part of me was screaming for me to touch her.

I wanted to taste, bite, and fuck every inch of her body.

"Show me." She looked down at my cock before running her pink tongue over her bottom lip. "Show me what you do when you think about me."

"Frankie."

"No one is here." Her hand was still moving in tiny little circles, and they moved more rapidly the more she spoke.

"You can't possibly be doing anything wrong if you're only touching yourself. I just want to watch."

Her words were like a fucking drug, and I couldn't resist their pull.

"Please, Olly. I don't want my only experience to be with him."

My chest felt like it was going to crack open as her eyes pleaded with me. There was no chance in hell that I was going to deny her. There was no fucking way that I would be able to tell her no after what she just said.

I reached out and pushed her hair over her left shoulder so I got a clearer view of her face, then I tried not to over-think things as I slowly undid my belt and popped the button on my jeans.

She was watching my every move as if it pushed her further and further, and I thought I was going to come in my hand as I pulled my cock out of my pants and listened to her whimper.

"Oh God." She closed her eyes and slammed her head back against the headrest as I began to move my hand. Her thighs were trembling beneath her touch, and I was desperate to feel that vibration against my tongue. I wanted to know every little movement of her body.

But more than anything, I was desperate to erase anyone from her memory but me.

"Tell me what you want." I barely recognized my voice as I spoke, but I was too far gone to worry about it.

"You." Her answer was instant. "I wish it was your hand touching me. I wish you were the one making me come."

I squeezed the tip of my cock in my fist and closed my eyes.

"I wish your mouth was on me. I wish I could taste you. I've never…"

I leaned across the seat and jerked her hand from her jeans. There was an instant mark of shock and anger across her face, but it disappeared the moment I brought her fingers to my mouth and slid them along my tongue.

She tasted better than I could imagine, and my hand moved faster as her wetness spread throughout my mouth.

"You taste so fucking good." I kissed the tip of her fingers, and she watched me, mesmerized.

"I want to taste you."

"Not tonight." I shook my head.

"Please," she begged me, and I almost caved. I would have given just about anything to watch my cock disappear between her lips. I knew how soft her tongue was from the kiss earlier, and I could imagine how lethal it would be against my cock.

I reached across the seat and wrapped my hands around her. It took nothing to lift her to me, and she settled against me with her back pressed against my chest and her chest pressed to the steering wheel.

My cock was settled between her thighs, and I could feel the heat of her through her jeans. She moved her hips against me, as desperate to feel me as I was to feel her.

"Olly," she moaned my name and pressed her head back against my shoulder before turning her face to meet mine.

I didn't allow myself to think as I kissed her. I just took what I had been wanting for so damn long. She kissed me back with just as much want. We were a clash of lips and teeth, and I nipped at her bottom lip as I allowed my hand to press against her stomach. I could feel her trembling beneath my touch.

I circled her belly button with my middle finger, and she sucked in a harsh breath. I didn't hesitate as I slid my hand lower and pushed my fingers beneath her jeans. I was met with how wet she was almost instantly, and I bit down on her shoulder as I thrust my hips forward.

She was soft, so damn soft, and so fucking wet. I pushed my fingers through her pussy and swirled her wetness around as I went.

"Please, Olly."

I pushed my fingers down against her clit and her loud moan filled my car. I didn't give her time to adjust to the feeling. I began to move against her clit, my hand as harsh as my hips beneath her. I was forcing her body down against mine, and she began to move against me with the same roughness.

"You have no idea how long I've wanted to do this." I lifted my left hand to her neck and used my thumb to force her face to mine. I sucked her bottom lip into my mouth before kissing her, hard. "I've thought about how fucking good your pussy would feel every day. I've never felt anything better."

She moaned against my mouth, and I moved my hand farther down and sank my middle two fingers into her. She started riding my hand as I pumped in and out of her and pressed the heel of my palm into her clit.

"I want you to fuck me." She ran her lips along mine.

Her words shocked me and tormented me. I buried my face in her neck as I moved my fingers faster inside of her. I wanted to fuck her more than I had ever wanted anything else, but I couldn't. Not tonight. Not like this.

Frankie deserved better.

She deserved better than I was giving her now, but there was no way I could stop.

"Not tonight." I shook my head and lapped at the skin of her neck. "Just let me give you this."

She didn't answer. She just began moving harder and faster against me, her body chasing the feeling I was giving her, and every move of her hips pushed me further and further to the edge.

My phone vibrated in my cupholder, the loud noise ringing out around us, but neither of us stopped. If anything, we chased the feeling of just the two of us even harder.

We were blocking out everything that existed outside of this moment, and God, it felt like a dream.

"I'm going to come, Olly." She pressed her head back against my shoulder, and I tightened my fingers on her throat. Her heart was hammering beneath my touch, and I matched my fingers to the rhythm as they pumped in and out of her.

I felt like we were racing, hunting a feeling that we had been desperately wanting from each other for far too long, and it was finally within our grasp. Her hands pushed into my thighs, her fingers digging into my jeans as she held on and rode me harder.

I was going to come, and she had barely even touched me.

She pressed her mouth to mine, and I kissed her. My fingers dug into her neck as my tongue caressed hers, and she cried out against my mouth as she tightened her thighs and her body tensed above me.

Her scream was muffled against my mouth as her orgasm raced through her, and I couldn't last another second. I came against her thighs and pressed my mouth down roughly against hers. I wasn't ready to give her up, to give up this feeling, so I kissed her until both of our breathing had calmed and my heart rate returned to some-what normal.

I ran my tongue over her bottom lip before slowly pulling away, and I searched her eyes as she stared at me. She looked so tired yet so damn blissful, and I knew I was looking at her the same way.

"Are you okay?" I asked just as the reality of what we had just done started to hit me.

Beck was going to kill me. He was going to hate me.

Frankie had been drinking, and she wasn't thinking clearly. I was a fucking idiot. I should have never allowed this to happen.

"I'm more than okay." She leaned forward and kissed me again. This one was slow and lazy and felt like she was trying to erase every thought that had just flooded me. "I've wanted this for so long."

"You've been drinking."

She raised her hand and pressed it against my mouth before I could continue. "Stop," she whispered against her hand. "Please give me at least a few minutes before you ruin this."

I tried to listen to what she was saying, but my mind was still racing with the thought that I should have regretted what we had just done. But I didn't.

Not even a little bit.

Even though I tried to force the feeling to come.

I knew that I should have. I should have been freaking out and demanding that Frankie get off me, but the feel of her against me was far too good. This felt like it was exactly where she was meant to be.

And even as my heart raced with the thought of what Beck would do, I didn't regret her.

"Do you have to go home now?" she murmured against her now slack fingers as she pressed her forehead against mine.

"We should," I whispered before kissing her fingertips that were still pressed against my mouth.

"I don't want to," she whispered back so quietly that I almost didn't hear her.

"I know. Me either." I gripped her jaw in my hand and brought her mouth back to mine. I kissed her until I was hard beneath her again.

"Let's get you home." I pressed a kiss to her forehead even as the dread of leaving this moment settled in my chest, and she nodded against my mouth.

CHAPTER 5
FRANKIE

I stepped onto the yacht behind my parents, Beck, and Josie, and took a deep breath. I hated the way I felt.

Not only was this their graduation party, a party that was celebrating the fact that Olly was going to be leaving soon, but I hadn't spoken to him in days.

It wasn't that he hadn't tried either. He had called me and text, and of course, he had been at my house with Beck. But I had avoided him as much as I possibly could.

I wasn't ready to face whatever it was he had to say to me. I would rather live in this awkward limbo with him for a little bit longer. It was better than him telling me that he regretted me.

Because deep down, I knew that he did.

"Frankie." My name was released on a gasp, and I turned around to face Olly's mother just as she reached out for my hands. "You look absolutely beautiful." She held my hands out wide to get a better look at me.

"Thank you." I smiled at her, and the urge to pull my

hands from hers and cross my arms over my chest was over-whelming.

I was wearing an emerald green simple silk dress that had the tiniest straps and a slit that ended mid-thigh. I had loved it when my mom and I went shopping back when I was more than excited to attend this party, but both Beck and my dad had reacted as if I was half-naked when I came down the stairs. And even though my mother refused to let me change, I suddenly felt vulnerable in a dress that I had once loved.

"You look lovely as well, Mrs. Warner."

She pulled me into her for a hug, and I tried to let some of my anxiety fall from my body. I had always liked Olly's mom, even though I didn't know her exceptionally well. His parents were wealthy, wealthier than most of the families in this town, and they were constantly traveling and working.

I used to wonder if that was why Olly and Carson spent so much time at our house instead of theirs, but I knew it was because Olly was almost always alone.

They were always gone, and even though he wouldn't admit it, he hated it.

I didn't blame him.

My house was always bustling with people and my parents, and I couldn't imagine it being any other way. I couldn't imagine the way Olly felt, but he had made his own family out of his friends.

Beck and Carson had become like his brothers, and I was asking him to risk that.

"That son of mine is around here somewhere." Mrs. Warner released me and looked over my shoulder. "Make sure he saves a dance for you tonight."

"Absolutely." I nodded, but I had no intentions of dancing with Olly. My only plan was to avoid him altogether.

Because all I could think about was the feel of his skin on mine. The way his hand had felt against my pussy, the way I had begged him to give me what I wanted.

And even though he did, I knew I should have never done that to him. I should have let him tell me no just one more time, but I had been drinking and felt bolder than normal.

I had felt desperate to let Olly erase every experience I had before him, because even though I could barely remember that night, I knew it was bad. I felt so disgusting when I thought about it, and I wanted Olly to obliterate that feeling from me. Because despite everything, Olly had become a safe place for me, and I trusted him explicitly.

But that didn't stop me from feeling like an idiot.

I moved farther onto the yacht and looked around for my parents. There were already so many people on board the boat, and I couldn't see a thing through the crowd. I attempted to push through them, my feet already aching in my heels, and grabbed an hors d'oeuvre from a tray as a waiter passed by.

I shoved the bite of food in my mouth as I looked around. This party was fancy. Too fancy for a bunch of teenagers graduating high school, but people with money spent it on stupid and frivolous things.

And they always spent money on things that made them look good.

"Hey, you." I turned at the sound of Olly's voice and barely managed to swallow my food as I stared at him. He was wearing a black suit that looked like it was molded to his body with a crisp white shirt underneath. His hair seemed darker somehow and there was a trace of stubble on his chin that made my stomach flip.

"Hi." I felt so awkward, and I never felt that way with Olly. Not before.

"You've been avoiding me." He was straight to the point as he stepped an inch closer to me, and I both loved and hated him for that fact.

"I've been busy." It was a lie, and we both knew it. Even when I was busy, I always made time for him.

"Or avoiding me." He tucked his hands into the pockets of his slacks and I grinned.

"That too."

He chuckled and rubbed his hand over his jaw. "Do you have a minute to talk?"

"Yeah." I nodded and stepped toward him just as someone sidled up to his side.

"Can you believe this is it?" Sarah, a girl who was graduating with them, wrapped her arms around Olly's neck before looking over at me. "Oh my God, Frankie. You look so beautiful."

"Thank you." I forced out the words and clenched my fists at my sides. I didn't have a problem with Sarah. She was a nice enough girl, but I couldn't fucking think straight when her hands were on him.

She let go of him before looking around the room in awe. "This party is amazing, Olly."

"Thanks." He nodded, and I knew that he hated the attention this party caused. This was his family's party. Not his. If it was up to him, he wouldn't have had one at all.

If it were up to him, he'd probably be celebrating with a surfboard and his boys.

She waved at one of her friends across the room before looking back at him. "Save a dance for me, yeah?"

"Sure." He didn't sound thrilled by the idea, and I knew that should have made me happy, but it didn't. I didn't want him with her at all.

His eyes never left me the entire time she was near, and as soon as she left, he took a step closer. "That talk?"

My heart hammered in my chest. "We can do it another time. This is your graduation party. Go have fun."

He stepped closer still and reached out to grab my hand before I could pull away. "I'd rather have fun with you."

"Olly." I shook my head because this wasn't a conversation I wanted to have here. Hell, I didn't want to have it at all. "Can't we just pretend like I didn't throw myself at you and act like nothing ever happened? We can go back to exactly like we were before."

Because even though I had felt like I was drowning in the things I couldn't say to him, it was better than this. Having Olly as my best friend was better than not getting him at all.

He pushed some hair out of my face before tugging my hand and forcing me closer to him. "We could." He nodded before leaning down to speak against my ear. "But I can't get the taste of you off my tongue. I can't think about anything other than you."

My gaze flew to his because it was the last thing I expected him to say. "What?" My voice tremored, and my pulse hammered against my neck.

"You drive me fucking crazy." He practically growled against my skin. "And this fucking dress." His hand moved to my side, and he tightened his fingers into the delicate fabric. "I've never seen anyone look so beautiful in all my life."

I couldn't breathe. I felt like I had been suffocating since the moment his lips had touched mine at that party, and there wasn't a chance of me coming up for air. Not now. Not after what he had just said.

"Beck." I said the one name that would have us both thinking clearly. Because even though I wanted Olly more than anything, I also didn't want to fuck up his relationship with my brother. I couldn't.

Because Beck trusted Olly with everything he was.

And we were betraying that trust.

"I know." Olly nodded and pulled away from me, but not before his hand tightened against my side almost to the point of pain. "We'll figure it out."

As soon as those words passed his lips, I spotted my brother and Josie headed in our direction. Beck hadn't said a word about Olly or I acting weird, and I knew that he didn't suspect a thing. I should have felt guilty over that fact, but the only thing I could bring myself to feel was relief.

If Beck didn't suspect us, then maybe Olly wouldn't stop.

That was the only thing that continued to run through my mind. Olly was still mine, and that was so fucked up.

"Who the fuck are all these people?" Beck asked as he clapped Olly on his shoulder.

"Fuck if I know." He rolled his eyes and grabbed two drinks off the tray of a passing waiter. He handed me one before talking again. "Some people my parents invited. I just have to smile and pretend like I remember that one time I met them."

"Better you than me." Josie laughed. "I'm just glad they didn't invite my dad."

"Never." Olly shook his head, and I knew that he was probably solely responsible for making sure they didn't. Olly could pretend to be a lot of things, but he would always be the most thoughtful person when it came to his friends.

"Are you all planning to go to the Clermont High party after this?" She looked over at me, and from the way she was watching me, I knew that she knew something was up. I hadn't told her. I couldn't.

I couldn't possibly expect her to lie to Beck for me. It wouldn't be fair.

And Beck couldn't know.

"Yeah. Probably," Olly answered at the same time I said, "I don't think so."

"Why not?" Olly turned toward me, and it didn't matter that all three of them were looking at me, he was the only one who mattered.

"I'm just not feeling it." I shrugged and took a sip of my drink.

"You should come." Beck nodded.

"Yeah." Josie smiled. "I'm sure Harry will be there. You told me he's been texting you."

Olly tensed at her words. Josie was right. Harry had been texting me, but I wasn't texting him back. Not really.

Not other than to be polite.

I shook my head. "There's nothing going on there."

"He's cute," Josie said just as Allie and Carson walked up beside me.

"Who's cute?" Allie asked and pulled me into a hug.

"Harry."

"Who's Harry?" Carson asked as he scrunched his brow.

"That guy from the party," Josie answered as I began to sweat. "The one who was hitting on Frankie."

"He wasn't really hitting on me."

"He most certainly was." Allie laughed.

"There is nothing going on with me and Harry," I said firmly, too firmly, and all of their eyes swung in my direction. *Great.*

"Okayyy." Beck bugged his eyes out dramatically, and I wanted the floor to open up and swallow me whole.

"I'm going to go to the bathroom." I didn't wait for them to respond before I quickly turned away and headed in the opposite direction of where they stood. I had no idea if I was headed toward the bathroom, but I knew I couldn't just stand there any longer.

"Frankie, wait up!" Allie called out behind me, and a moment later, she wrapped her arm in mine. "Are you okay?"

"Yep," I answered quickly but kept walking.

"You should work on that answer because it wasn't very believable." She chuckled and pulled my arm until I was forced to walk to the left. "Come on. The bathroom is this way."

I let her lead me to the bathroom, and I snuck a glance behind me to where we had just left the others. Olly's gaze connected with mine almost instantly. He was watching me, searching for something, and I didn't know what he wanted.

I never really knew when it came to him.

And right now, I felt even more confused than ever before because I desperately wanted him, but I also knew that he was capable of hurting me more than anyone else ever had.

We pushed through the bathroom door, and I walked directly to the sink. I held on to the sides while I tried to catch my breath, and when I finally looked up at myself in the mirror, Allie was standing behind me with a soft look on her face.

"Do you want to tell me what happened?"

"No." I shook my head, but my body vibrated with the need to talk about it with someone.

"You know that Josie and I are always here for you."

"I can't tell Josie." I shook my head and winced. Josie was one of my best friends. She and Allie both were, and it made me feel like shit that I was purposely keeping something from either of them.

"Okay." Allie nodded and stepped closer to me as she lowered her voice. "We don't have to say anything to her if you don't want to." She reached up and fixed a piece of my hair that ran down my back. "But I'm assuming that means this has to do with Olly."

"Doesn't it always?"

"Yeah." She chuckled. "I guess it does." Her eyes met mine in the mirror, and she gave me a few minutes before she spoke again. "What happened?"

"I don't know." I shook my head and turned on the cold water before running my fingers beneath. "He drove me home from the party the other night, and..."

"And?"

"And I basically threw myself at him." I shut off the water and turned toward her. "When he clearly didn't want to touch me, I started touching myself," I whispered the last part, and I hated the way she gasped then tried to hide her grin. "This is not funny, Allie. That's embarrassing."

She rolled her eyes and reached for a paper towel. "No. It's not." She was thoughtful for a second before she looked back at me. "Unless he wasn't affected by it."

"No." I nodded my head even despite my answer. "He was definitely affected by it. He... he touched me and said things I never expected to hear him say."

"So, what's the problem?"

"Really?" I held my hands out as if that said everything. "He's Beck's best friend, and he would kill him if he ever found out."

"I don't think that's true. Not if he knew how much you loved each other."

"Oh my God." I laughed. "I do not love him, and he most certainly does not love me." Only part of that was a lie.

"Well, you're wrong about that, but I'll let you have it for now." She moved around me and pulled some lipstick out of her small clutch. "You know he's leaving, though, right. He's going to be gone with Carson soon."

"Of course, I do." It was all I could freaking think about.

"Then let it be a fling. A summer lo... hookup." She ran the lipstick over her lips before turning back to me. "Just have fun."

Fun. Because at the end of all of this, he was leaving regardless of what happened between us, and fun meant I wouldn't get my heart broken.

"Beck doesn't need to know anything." She shrugged her shoulders as if it were that simple. "If you want to be with Olly and have this last summer together before he's off to college, then have it. Beck doesn't get to have a say in it if you don't let him."

"So, we keep it a secret from everyone?"

"Just a pretty lie." She shrugged. "Your only other options are to tell Beck the two of you want to be together or let it go completely."

"I don't even know if Olly actually wants this."

"Oh, honey." She linked her arm in mine again and led me out of the bathroom. "The only people who haven't noticed how badly Olly wants you is you and your idiot brother."

I took a deep breath as I thought about what she had just said. A secret affair with one of my best friends. Was I okay with that? I honestly wasn't sure, but I knew that the alternative felt like torture. If Olly wasn't ready to pursue this, and I honestly wasn't sure that he would ever be, would I be okay with staying like we were?

If a pretty lie with Olly was all I could get, then I knew I would take it.

The loud noise of the party greeted us as soon as we stepped out of the bathroom, but I spotted Olly almost instantly. He was leaning against the railing with a drink in his hand, and he was still staring at me like he had been waiting his whole life for me.

My stomach flipped, and I let Allie's words rush through me. Me and him. No one else has to know.

It would be our secret to keep.

"Go on." Allie pressed her hand on my back and gave me a small shove in Olly's direction.

He smiled at me as I made my way toward him, and it was so unfair how damn handsome he looked. He took a sip of his drink as he watched me, and I had never felt so self-conscious in front of him before.

But now, it was like every small look from him mattered more than it had before.

"What are you doing over here by yourself?" I leaned against the railing beside him and tried to act normal. "Isn't this supposed to be your party?"

"That's what they say." He never let his gaze venture from me. "But there's really only one person I'm interested in seeing."

"Have you always been this good at this?"

"At what?" He laughed and cocked his head.

"That." I waved toward his face, and his smile deepened.

"Well, I'm not really sure what you're referring to, but I'm going to go with yes."

"Uh-huh."

"Speaking of things I'm good at." He leaned in closer as if what he was telling me was top secret. "My mother tells me that I'm supposed to be saving a dance for you tonight, and I'm absolutely dying to." I swallowed hard as he kept going. "Do you think we can knock out two birds with one stone?"

"Is that your way of asking me to dance?" My voice was so rough it was barely recognizable. I pressed my thighs together and willed myself not to be turned on simply by him saying he wanted to dance with me.

But it was a useless attempt.

"It's my way of asking you to do fucking anything that will allow me to touch you for even a second." I watched as his fist clenched around his glass, and I was worried it might break.

I tried to think of what to say, of how to respond to him, but nothing came. The only thought that kept going through my mind was yes. Yes. Absolutely yes.

"I'm not sure I can take another moment without it."

I blinked up at him and tried not to let him see how affected I was by his words. "You've gone a very long time without touching me before."

"That was before I knew."

"Knew what?" I felt like I could barely breathe.

He leaned in closer and gripped my fingers in his. "What it was like to have you on my fingers. To have you moaning my name."

"Olly," I whispered his name because I didn't know what else to say. I had never experienced him like this before. I had never heard him speak so openly.

I had never seen him look at me the way he was looking at me now, and I wondered if he felt the same. If we were truly seeing each other for the first time.

"Let's dance." He tugged me toward the dance floor, and for the first time since I got next to him, I remembered that there were other people in the room.

I tried to calm my breathing as we passed by others, but he didn't seem to care about any of them. He stopped right in the middle of the makeshift dance floor, and he smiled as he turned toward me and tugged me into his body.

My chest pressed into his, and I only hesitated for a moment before I lifted my hands to his shoulders. I rested them there lightly, so unsure of what I was supposed to do, but he pressed his fingers just above my elbows and let his fingers run over my skin until they met my hands.

"Here." He wrapped my fingers around his neck, and I tightened my grip there. "Your hands go here." He let his fingers trail back down my arms before dropping them to my hips. Every inch of my skin felt like it was on fire from his touch. "And my hands go here."

His hands tightened, and he tugged me impossibly closer as he began to move us along the floor.

"Where's my brother?"

"He went to get some food." He didn't pull his attention away from me for a second. "But we're not doing anything wrong, Frankie."

Part of me thought he was trying to convince himself of that fact more than me.

"And what about what we did the other night?"

"Well." He swallowed hard, and I could practically see the thoughts racing through his head. I stared straight ahead at his throat as I feared what he would say next. Because I knew there was only one answer.

"We don't have to tell anyone." I blurted it out so suddenly I shocked both of us.

"I would never ask that of you." He shook his head, and I knew he was being honest. Olly was the best guy I had ever met.

"You didn't." I shook my head and almost tripped over my feet.

Olly caught me against his body and continued to move us effortlessly.

"But you're leaving soon," I repeated the reasoning Allie had given me in the bathroom. "And this doesn't have to be anything more than what we make it."

He stared down at me for a long second. "Do you really believe that?"

Of course, I didn't. I knew that no matter what happened with Olly, I would be completely and utterly wrecked after.

But that didn't stop me from wanting it.

I wasn't sure if there would ever be anything that could stop me from wanting him.

I would face the consequences when they came.

"What other choice do we have?" I tightened my hands around his neck.

He hesitated for a second, but then he stared into my eyes with so much determination that it made my stomach flip. "I could tell Beck."

Within an instant, my stomach sank. Every little butterfly that had been fluttering only a moment before had all but disappeared. Because I knew that even though Olly was willing to fuck up his friendship with Beck over this, I wasn't willing to let him go through with it.

Not for this. Not for me.

"No." I shook my head and pulled my gaze away from him long enough to look for my brother, but I didn't see him anywhere. "Not like this. Not now. Let's just see where things go, then we'll tell them."

"So what? You want me to be your dirty little affair?" He grinned and spun me around the dance floor.

"No." I laughed and hung on for dear life. "I just don't want you to lose your best friend over something that might only last the summer."

The smile dropped from his face, and I knew he was thinking about what I just said. And he knew I was right. What we had done wasn't worth telling Beck. Not yet if what Allie said was right. This could just be the best summer of my life, and no one had to know. We didn't have to ruin friendships or trust, and I would do everything in my power to protect my heart from him.

That was the only choice that I had.

It was a choice I was going to make. I would choose Olly over almost anything.

"So, just the summer? What're the rules here?" He cocked an eyebrow.

"Rules." I tapped my fingers against his neck as I thought. "This ends when the summer does, no one knows but us, and we don't make it complicated."

He stared down at me for a long moment, and I thought he was going to tell me no. "We lie to Beck?"

I shrugged my shoulders like it was no big deal. "We lie to everyone. Just for the summer."

There was so much hesitation in his eyes, and I was

surprised when the next words left his lips. "Okay. Just for the summer."

I took a deep breath and my hands trembled at his neck as my heart raced.

"Look." Olly pointed to the edge of the yacht where people were gathering, and I saw the first burst of light as it flashed over their heads. "The fireworks are starting."

Olly gripped my fingers in his and tugged me to the far end of the boat where there was far less of a crowd. I pressed my stomach against the railing as I looked out over the water, then back to where the fireworks were beginning to go off. Olly stood behind me, his chest pressed against my back, both of his hands holding onto the railing at my sides.

"Your parents must be really happy you graduated," I joked as I looked back over my shoulder at him. "There must've been a time when they really doubted it would happen."

Olly laughed and looked down at me, and the urge to lean up on my tiptoes just the slightest bit and kiss him was overwhelming. That was the only thing I would miss, the thing I would crave, being able to touch him, to kiss him with everybody watching. The urge to make sure everyone knew that he belonged to me even when he didn't.

"I think my parents just take every opportunity they can to pretend that they're something they're not," he said the words so easily, like they didn't bother him at all, but they didn't sit right with me. I absolutely hated that they weren't everything he needed them to be.

"I wish I could touch you right now," I confessed before looking away from him and staring back out at the fireworks that were now booming and cracking through the sky. The display was beautiful, and only more so as it reflected off the dark ocean below.

Olly leaned in closer to me, his chest pressing fully against my back and forcing my stomach into the railing. "You are touching me." He leaned down till he was talking almost directly in my ear. "But I can touch you more if that's what you want."

I looked around, but not a single person was paying attention to us. Everyone was mesmerized and in awe of the show in front of us, and the next crack of a firework made me jump as my stomach began to tremble.

"What?" I didn't turn back toward him. I just continued to stare out, but all I could think about was what he had just said.

I watched as his fingers dropped from the railing, and I held my breath as I anticipated his next move. I startled when his warm fingertips pressed against my thigh just to where the slit began in my dress.

His pointer finger toyed with the fabric there, and he might as well have stripped me bare with that one move. I felt like everyone could see exactly what he was doing, like they could see the way my chest rose and fell with desperate need. But no one was paying any attention to us at all.

"You look so goddamn beautiful tonight," he practically growled against my shoulder. "Has anyone told you that?"

I didn't answer him because I didn't trust my voice. I simply shook my head and concentrated on the way his finger was now moving in tiny circles. He dipped it below the fabric just on the inside of my thigh, and I sucked in a sharp breath.

I had never done anything like this before. But there was something about the thought that anyone could easily catch us that made my heart race in a way that I knew I would never be able to find this feeling with anyone else.

This had nothing to do with the people around us and everything to do with him.

"Do you want this?" He didn't wait for my answer before he continued. "Do you want me to touch you where any of these fucking people can see?"

I couldn't answer him because I could barely breathe. But he didn't stop. His fingers moved higher and higher so slowly that I wanted to scream from the ache that was building between my legs.

He pressed his fingers to the apex of my thighs, and I tightened my hands on the railing in front of me as his finger finally met the fabric of my panties. He toyed with me, moving his finger ever so lightly against that thin piece of lace that kept us apart.

"Are you already wet?" His voice was so low I barely heard the words, but I nodded my head as I squeezed my thighs together against his finger.

"I need to feel it," he groaned before sliding my panties to the side and dipping his fingers beneath. My thighs shook as he slid lower and lower, and he moaned against the back of my neck when he was met with how turned on I was.

"God," he said the word so loudly that anyone could hear him, but still no one seemed to be paying us any attention. He leaned down closer to me, his mouth hovering just above my ear as he said, "I feel like I'm going to die if I don't taste you." His finger met my clit, and my hips surged forward as he continued. "I'd love to lay you out on one of these tables and fuck you with my mouth."

I looked around as my chest heaved before quickly

looking back at him. "Olly, there are so many people around."

"I don't care about any of these people." His fingers moved faster, and I clenched my eyes shut as I tried to hold off the orgasm that was building far too quickly. "Do you think they know?"

I opened my eyes to look up at his that were staring at me so possessively.

"Know what?"

"That you are going to come on my fingers right beside them. That while they are in awe of these stupid fucking fireworks in the sky, I'm watching you fall apart under my touch. Every single person I shake hands with later, I'll be doing it with traces of your cum all over my fingers."

"Oh my God," I whispered and fell back into his chest. My thighs were already shaking, and he was barely even touching me. His filthy words were like an extra set of hands tracing over my body and touching me in places I couldn't even see.

His fingers moved off my clit going lower and lower until he pushed inside of me, and I had nowhere to move. I couldn't widen my legs to give him better access, and everything felt so incredibly tight. His palm pushed into my clit as he forced his fingers in and out.

My body felt so damn tight as my orgasm began to build inside of me like a tsunami. It was all-consuming and rapid, and I had no control. I tried to hold it off because there were so many people around us, but Olly was having none of that.

He pumped faster and pressed harder, and when he leaned down and whispered in my ear, I didn't stand a chance.

"Let go," he demanded of me. "Be a good girl and give me what's mine."

I came on his fingers as if his command had simply pulled it from me. I pressed my hand to my mouth as a scream started climbing up my too-dry throat, and I bit down on my palm. The pain in my hand mixed with the pleasure from his, and I had no idea how I remained standing.

It was too much.

He was too much, but he didn't let me fall. He stood firmly against me as I rode out my orgasm, and only when I could finally breathe again, did he pull his hand away from my pussy.

He turned me to face him just as the last few fireworks cracked in the air, and I watched him as he lifted his hand and placed his middle two fingers into his mouth. He ran his tongue along the bottom, tasted me on his skin, and my knees threatened to buckle again.

He pulled his hand away from his mouth and gently pushed a piece of my hair over my shoulder with those same fingers. "Come on. Everyone is probably looking for us, and you need some food."

CHAPTER 6
OLLY

I watched Frankie as she laughed with Josie and Allie and spun in a circle on the dance floor. She was happy. Happier than I had seen her in a long time, and I knew that a big part of that had to do with me. With us, and guilt slammed into my chest.

Because no matter what happened between us this summer, I would be leaving at the end of it, and I didn't want her happiness to be reliant on me. I didn't want her to feel trapped in what we became.

"Are we going to that party tonight?" Carson leaned back in his chair with his eyes still on Allie.

"Yeah. I have to deal with all this shit first." I waved my hand around the yacht. "My parents will lose their shit if I just bounce."

"Ah." Carson and Beck both looked over to where my parents were talking to a crowd of people. "Mr. And Mrs. Warner are really laying it on thick tonight, aren't they?"

"Of course, they are. Their pride and joy is graduating

high school." I couldn't help rolling my eyes as I lifted my drink to my lips.

"They still pissed about California?" Beck pressed his elbows into the table and leaned closer to me.

"Furious is more like it. I'm honestly surprised they haven't called the recruiter and threatened to sue them."

"So, they're still cutting you off?"

"That's the threat." I shrugged my shoulders like it didn't matter, but the thought scared me to death. I would get a job and provide for myself. I wasn't afraid of work, but I was worried about how it would affect the hours I could put into my game. And right now, doing well on that damn team and going pro were the only things that mattered.

Because if I didn't, my parents would be right.

I was wasting my damn life chasing a dream that was never going to happen instead of doing exactly what they had planned for me. And I knew that following in their footsteps to work at their investment firm was a life that would provide me more than I could ever want, but I couldn't imagine ever wanting it at all. Their life.

All they did was work. That was their love. Not each other. Not me.

And I didn't fucking want that.

"You know my dad will give you money," Beck offered, and I loved him for it. I loved his dad too, and I knew that he would with no questions asked. But that was the last thing I wanted.

"No." I shook my head. "If they're going to cut me off, then that's fine. I'll just have to prove to them that I'm not making a mistake."

Carson and Beck looked back and forth between each

other, and I knew that they probably thought I was, but it didn't matter. I didn't want to be anything like my parents.

It was why the three of us had made the pact to leave for college in the first place.

"Part of me wishes I was still going with you all." Beck chuckled before his eyes searched out Josie. "God knows we'd get into some trouble."

"I think you're going to have plenty of trouble on your own." Carson laughed and slapped him on the shoulder. "Your hands are going to be full. That's for sure."

"What about you?" I nodded to Carson. "How are you feeling about leaving Allie?"

The smile dropped from his face, and he ran his fingers through his hair. "I hate it, but we'll be fine. We're going to visit each other as much as we can, and you better get yourself some earplugs so you don't have to listen to our Face-Time sex."

Beck chuckled just as Allie walked up behind Carson and wrapped her arms around his shoulders. "What are you all talking about?"

"Nothing," Beck answered just as Carson said, "Me and you fucking over a phone screen."

I couldn't help but laugh at the shock on Allie's face just before she smacked Carson in the back of the head.

"Ow." He laughed and rubbed the spot before hooking his hand behind her neck and pulling her down for a kiss. If she was still angry with him, she didn't show it. She melted against him within a second, and I made a mental note to order a bulk supply of earplugs ASAP.

"Get a room," Josie teased as she and Frankie joined us at the table.

Frankie took the seat next to me, and even though I

expected it to feel awkward, there wasn't a trace of it. Her knee bumped into mine gently before she quickly moved it away, and I couldn't stop myself from reaching under the table and wrapping my fingers around her bare knee until I forced it back against mine.

Her gaze snapped to mine for a quick second before she looked away, but I kept my hand there, rubbing tiny circles on her skin.

"Are you all about ready to head out?" Beck wrapped his arm around Josie's waist and pulled her toward him.

"Yeah. Whenever you are." Josie looked over at me with a smile. "This was fun, Olly."

"This was pretentious." I said what we were all thinking. "But I'm glad you all were here for it."

"Hey, guys." I looked up just as my mom walked up to the table and smiled at everyone. "Are you having fun?"

I tightened my hand on Frankie's thigh without thinking.

"Yes. Thank you for having us." Beck nodded.

"Of course." My mom acted like her hosting my friends was no big deal, but it was. My friends were never around my parents. Hell, I barely was myself. "We're just so proud of you all."

"Thank you." This time it was from Carson.

"Do you care if I steal Olly away for a bit? I have some people I need him to rub elbows with." My mom smiled, but I wasn't smiling back at her. I didn't want to rub elbows with any of her people. I just wanted to get off this damn boat and be with my friends. I wanted to go get lost in Frankie.

Frankie, who now had her fingers wrapped around mine against her leg. "Actually, Mrs. Warner, Olly promised me another dance first. Can he come to find you after?"

"Sure." My mom smiled, but I could see the small tick of

annoyance in her face that I wasn't jumping to do exactly what she wanted.

Frankie and I stood from the table just as Josie spoke. "Thank you again for having us. I think Beck and I are going to head out."

My mom pulled Josie into a hug, and to anyone else, it probably looked genuine. It just made me want to get away from her that much more.

I tugged Frankie toward the dance floor as the rest of them said their goodbyes, and I tried not to think about anything other than her.

"What's going on up there?" Frankie softly tapped her finger against my temple, and I pulled my attention away from where we had just left and looked back down at her.

"Nothing." I shook my head, but we both knew that was a lie.

She didn't take my answer seriously for a single moment. "Is it about your mom?"

"Maybe it's about you." I twirled her around until neither one of us was facing them.

"What did I do?" She scrunched her brow. "I've been nothing but nice tonight."

"Yeah." I nodded and leaned down to speak into her ear. "But you look so goddamn beautiful in that dress that I just want to rip it off you."

She blushed and looked away from me before bringing her gaze back to meet mine. "You're just trying to change the subject."

"You might be right." I shrugged before staring down at the soft curve of her neck. "But it's the fucking truth."

Her blush crept up her neck as she brought her gaze

back to meet mine. "You've never talked to me like this before."

I thought about what she was saying, and she was right. "I wasn't allowed to before."

"Technically..." She brought her soft hand up my chest and hooked it around my neck. "I don't think you're allowed to now either." She chuckled, and the sound was so fucking sweet.

My hands tightened around her waist, and I knew the fabric of her dress would be wrinkled beneath my touch. "I don't think anyone but you and I really have much of a say in it anymore."

She looked over to where her brother and the rest of our friends were leaving, and I could see the hesitancy on her face. Despite what she said, she wasn't sure about this.

"We don't have to do this," I whispered close to her ear, and her gaze snapped back to meet mine.

"And what?" She blinked up at me. "Just go back to what we were before?"

"No." I shook my head as I tried to imagine what it would be like not to be able to touch her again. "Unless that's what you want." She opened her mouth to say something, but I couldn't stop the words from rolling past my lips. "But I don't know how I'm supposed to be near you anymore without touching you now that I know exactly what you feel like when you're coming against my fingers. But if that's what you want, I will try."

"You know that's not what I want." She shook her head too and her hand tightened around my neck. "I'm just worried about him."

"I know." I nodded. I was worried about him too. Because as desperate as I felt to have Frankie, I was also desperate not to lose him. He was my family. They all were. "But we'll deal with that later. Right now is about you and me and this summer."

"Okay." She smiled and pressed her chest against mine. "You and me."

"And a room full of people who are currently watching us," I whispered, and she chuckled as she looked around.

Sure enough, almost everyone still on this damn yacht was looking our way, but I couldn't bring myself to care. Not when I spotted her parents or mine watching us.

"We do make a really cute couple." I tucked a piece of hair behind her ear, and the urge to lean down and kiss her was overwhelming.

"A cute non-couple."

"Sure." I grinned and spun her until her body was shielded by mine. "If that's the title you want to give us."

"And what would you call us, Mr. Warner?"

"I don't know yet." I was honest with her. "But I do know that I'm dying for us to get out of here. Do you think we can make a break for it?"

She grinned harder until both the dimples were visible on her cheeks, and I desperately wanted to trace them with my tongue. "Well, I'm wearing heels and I'm already pretty clumsy, so there is a good chance we won't make it out."

"I'll carry you if need be."

"You wouldn't dare." She laughed just as I reached down and scooped my arm beneath her knees. I lifted her with no issue as she wrapped her arms fully around my neck.

"Now everyone is really looking."

She was right, of course. Everyone was watching us as I strode toward the exit, and I could see the disapproval in my mother's eyes before she even began making her way over to us. She caught us just in time before we stepped off the yacht, and the fake smile on her face almost made me sick.

"Olly," she called out my name as she stepped toward us, and I held Frankie tighter against me. She wiggled for me to let her down, but I refused. I just tightened my hold on her and pulled her closer to my chest. "I told you there are some people I'd like you to talk to before you leave."

"And I told you earlier that I didn't want to talk to any of these people."

I felt Frankie tense against me, and I didn't blame her. The tone I was using with my mother was enough to make anyone feel awkward, but this was a conversation we'd had over and over and over again. I wasn't here to entertain her guests or to make sure they all knew my face and name. That's what she was here for. That was her goal.

And we'd already had this conversation before we even left the damn house.

"You don't really have a choice." She looked over her shoulder, and I knew she was probably smiling at someone to keep up all the pretenses of the loving mother she pretended to be. "Your father's waiting for you."

I opened my mouth to tell her that I didn't care what my father was waiting for, but Frankie spoke before I could.

"Do you care if I come along?" Frankie smiled gently at my mother. "My date for tonight stood me up, and your son has promised to spend the entire night with me to make sure I forget." She patted my chest gently.

"Of course not." My mother's hand tightened around her glass, and I knew this wasn't what she wanted. But if she wanted me over there, she was going to take both of us. If it wasn't for Frankie, I would have already walked out. "But do you mind walking, or does Olly need to carry you everywhere?"

Frankie wiggled in my hands again, and I knew she was embarrassed by my mother's comment. I wasn't. There was only one person whose opinion mattered when it came to me and Frankie, and he was already gone.

"I'd prefer to carry her, but if you insist." I placed Frankie back to her feet gently and whispered against her neck so my mother couldn't hear, "I get a much better view of your ass this way anyway."

Frankie smacked my chest before I chuckled and placed her hand in mine. We followed my mother as she led us back toward where my father stood, and I used Frankie's hand in mine to try to steady my nerves.

"There he is!" my father cheered as he wrapped his arm around my shoulders and pulled me into his side. I didn't loosen my grip on Frankie, and truth be told, I wasn't sure if I could. I needed her here more than she knew.

"Congratulations, Oliver." One of the men standing around my father raised his glass in my direction and I nodded.

"So, what're the big plans now? Are you coming to your dad's company?"

"He needs to sow his wild oats first." My dad laughed and clamped down on my shoulder. "Play ball and meet some girls. You know how it goes."

The men around us chuckled, and I felt Frankie tense beside me. My dad was right, but he was also wrong. Baseball wasn't some wild hair I needed to get out of the way. I was in love with the sport, and it was what I wanted to do. Whether he could see that or not was irrelevant.

But I wasn't going away to college for the girls.

"I'm actually hoping to go pro." I looked up at the man who had just asked even though I didn't know his name. "I'm not planning on working for my dad's company if I can help it."

I watched as the anger streaked across my father's face, and I tensed for his reaction. "Wishful thinking, boys." He laughed and took a long swig of the dark liquor in his hand. "Didn't all of us think we were good enough to do the same once upon a time?"

Which meant he didn't think I was.

It was nothing new. He told me this more often than I could count, but the more the words passed his lips the harder the resolve inside of me to prove myself became.

As they all laughed, Frankie's hand tightened in mine.

I looked down at her, and she shot me a small smile before leaning into my shoulder. "We should get out of here. I feel like going for a swim."

She looked so damn beautiful looking up at me, and my chest ached as I looked at her.

"Baseball is good for the ladies, son, but eventually they're going to be looking at your wallet."

I wasn't sure who said that, but there was another round of laughter that followed his words. I didn't look away from Frankie even as she scrunched up her nose in disgust.

"A swim sounds wonderful."

I heard my father call my name, but I didn't stop as I pulled Frankie as far from them as we could go. She held the edge of her dress in her hand as she jogged behind me, and her laughter echoed around me.

We stepped off the yacht and onto the ramp that led down to the long dock.

"Your mom is watching us." Frankie looked over her shoulder before turning back to me.

"I honestly don't fucking care."

We stepped onto the dock, and I forced myself not to look back to where I knew she'd be. We walked past row after row of obnoxious yachts that were parked far more than they were used, and I finally took a deep breath when my Oxfords pushed into the sand.

"This way." I nodded toward the beach, and Frankie stopped to slip her heels from her feet. She collected them in her hand before she smiled at me without a single worry.

She skipped in front of me, spinning around to face me, and the soft wind off the ocean blew her hair and dress around her. "I don't know how you deal with that." She nodded to the yacht that was still lit up like a Christmas tree. It was far enough away that I could no longer see the people on the boat that I didn't give a shit about.

"I barely even notice it anymore." I shrugged and pulled my jacket off my shoulders.

"Yes. You do." She tossed her heels down in the sand before twirling in a circle with her arms held out. She closed her eyes as she took a deep breath, and I desperately wanted to know what was running through her mind. "And I hate that they treat you that way."

I laid my jacket down just out of reach of the wet sand and took a seat beside it. I patted the fabric for her to sit, but she simply rolled her eyes and dropped to her knees in front of me. She braced herself with her hands on my knees as she smiled softly at me.

"Pretty soon I'll be gone, and they won't have much of a say anymore."

The smile dropped from her face instantly, and I felt like

an asshole for bringing it up. "Is that why you decided to go all the way to California?"

"I mean, yes and no." I lifted my hand and traced my finger along hers. "At first, the guys and I just decided on California as a point on the map because we all wanted to get away. Then our idea sounded even better because we could still surf."

She rolled her eyes, and I couldn't help but chuckle.

"But then their baseball team became the real reason we wanted to go. It's a good fucking program, and the coach is amazing."

"And you'll do amazing there." She stared down at where my hands were touching hers.

"I hope so." I ran my finger over the thin gold band she wore on her pointer finger. "If not, they'll just be right."

"They aren't." She shook her head. "Even if you don't go pro like you were talking about up there, that doesn't make them right."

"You have too much faith in me."

"No. I don't. I just know you." She leaned forward and her gaze dropped to my lips. "I know what you're capable of."

"I wish I wasn't going to California." My words were barely loud enough for either of us to hear, but they shocked me to my core. I didn't know what I was saying. I was going. I wanted to go. I just didn't want to leave her.

"I know." She nodded gently, but her gaze didn't sway. "But how will you sow your wild oats if you don't?"

I snorted and rolled my eyes before wrapping my fingers around her sides and tugging her closer to me. "I can think of a few ways."

"Show me," she whispered, and I wasted no time catching her lips against mine.

I kissed her like I had been frantic to do all night.

I pulled her forward between my thighs, and she ran her fingers through my hair as she kissed me back. This kiss wasn't as rushed or urgent as the last time we kissed, but it felt just as consuming.

Her lips moved over mine gently, exploring, and I ran my tongue over her bottom lip because I was dying for a taste. She opened for me, and the anticipation of tasting her again was enough to make my breath catch in my throat.

Her kiss was full of fire, but it still calmed me somehow. She steadied me and impassioned me at the same time.

It was as if everything she was giving had always belonged to me, and I was desperate to get it back.

My hands tightened along her sides as I pulled her closer to me and bit down on her bottom lip. She moaned, the tiniest whimper that was lost to the loud crash of the waves behind her, but the sound raced through me like a drug.

Her dress rose higher and higher against her thighs, and her breaths rose and fell against my chest in a rush. I wanted her. More than I had ever wanted anything else in my life, and my hands shook as I pulled her impossibly closer to me still.

I kissed along her jaw before nipping her soft earlobe with my teeth, and I let my tongue roll over the small jewel that decorated her ear.

"You taste like fucking sin." I kissed below her ear and made my way down her neck. "I can't wait to taste your sweet little pussy."

She moaned again, and this time, I ran my teeth over her exposed collarbone.

"Please, Olly."

"You look so beautiful tonight." I pressed a gentle kiss to the curve of her perfect breast. "And you deserve someone who is going to treat you gently, but everything I want to do to you is beyond disrespectful."

She trembled against me, and I ran my tongue beneath the fabric of her dress. I brought my fingers to her inner thigh, and I ran them over the soft skin there.

"I want to devour every fucking part of you until you can't remember anyone other than me. Years from now when you touch your pussy, I want my name to be the first sound on your lips."

"Oh God." She leaned closer to me, her pussy begging to be touched.

"Is that what you want, Frankie?" I gripped her thigh in my hand roughly and her breath left her in a rush. "Because I've wanted you for so fucking long that I'm not sure I'll be able to stop once I get a taste."

She nodded her head, but that wasn't enough.

"Tell me."

"Yes. God, yes. Please." She tugged on the strands of my hair until she forced my face back up to hers, and I kissed her just as I planned to do with her pussy.

I lifted my hand up her thigh and met the soft fabric of her panties. She gasped against my mouth as I slipped my finger inside and felt how wet she was.

I pushed my middle finger inside her before pushing the moisture around her clit, and she tensed on her knees in front of me. Pulling my hand from her panties, I broke our kiss and brought my hand to her mouth.

"Taste," I instructed her, and I saw the hesitation in her

eyes. "Taste how fucking perfect you are. I want to taste you off your lips before I taste you from your pussy."

Her eyes met mine as she opened her mouth and let me push my finger inside. Her tongue rolled against my skin as her gaze darkened, and she sucked my finger farther into her mouth.

My cock strained against my slacks as I watched her, and she didn't dare let her gaze stray from mine. She stared at me as she cleaned every last drop of her from my finger, and it was the hottest fucking thing I had ever seen.

I ripped my finger from her mouth before wrapping them in her hair and jerking her forward. This kiss was rushed and frantic, and I groaned when the taste of her hit my tongue.

I lifted her, wrapping her thighs around mine before I flipped her over onto her back. She arched her back as her head pressed down into my jacket, and I slipped the thin strap of her dress from her shoulder.

The fabric fell away from her breast and revealed that she wore no bra beneath. I captured her nipple in my mouth as I wrapped my arm beneath her back. I held her to me as I teased her with my tongue and had her squirming with my teeth.

She let her thighs fall open on either side of me and my hips settled perfectly against hers. I knew that she could feel how hard I was against her, and I felt like I was going to come apart when she raised her hips to meet mine.

I sat up on my knees and stared down at her beneath me. She was too fucking beautiful, too pure, and I knew that I didn't deserve to touch her. But I also knew that there was absolutely no chance of me walking away from her either.

"I need you." She squirmed against me, and my gaze fell

to her thighs. Her emerald dress was pushed up to the tops of her thighs, and I could see the thin, black panties that it hid.

"I'm going to take care of you." I pressed my fingers into the inside of her knees and jerked them farther apart until they were pressed into the sand at her sides. Her legs trembled under my touch, and she arched up off the ground farther as she watched me. "Now be a good girl and lie back while I eat this pussy." I ran my fingers over the black fabric, and she pressed the back of her hand against her mouth as she watched me.

Tucking my fingers in the top of the fabric, I yanked it forward, causing her hips to lift from the ground slightly and the fabric to rip under my touch. She was so fucking wet, and I pressed my hands against her thighs, holding her open as I stared down at her.

"Olly." She squirmed as I took in every inch of her perfect body.

"Watch me." I lowered my head closer to her and ran my tongue over my bottom lip. "Don't take your fucking eyes off me for a second, Frankie."

Her gaze slammed into mine, and I pressed a soft kiss against her pussy. She slid her hand down her body quickly, and she tugged on her dress as if she was going to cover herself. I could see the timidness in her eyes staring back at me.

"That's not happening." I gripped her hand in mine and pressed it into her stomach as I ran my tongue through her folds. "You don't hide anything from me, Frankie. This is mine."

She nodded just as I flattened my tongue against her clit.

I dove into her pussy, tasting every inch of her, and her

hips rose and fell against my mouth. I settled between her thighs and snaked one arm beneath her left leg. Pressing my hand against her hip to keep her in place, I sucked her clit into my mouth as I brought my other hand to her opening.

She whimpered and tensed around me, and I slid a finger inside her. She was so ready for me, and I groaned against her pussy as her want coated my hand.

"Olly," she moaned my name, and her fingers laced through my hair.

I pumped my finger inside her, slowly at first before picking up speed, and I kept my gaze on hers as I assaulted her pussy with my tongue, lips, and teeth. She bit down on her lip as she stared down at me, and I added another finger before curling them inside of her.

"I want to touch you." She pushed up on her elbow and her other hand clung to the back of my head.

"Not tonight," I said before sucking on her clit again. "Tonight, I just want to taste you. I want to feel you come against my tongue like I've imagined so many times."

She dropped back to the sand with a moan, and I continued to eat her like I was starving. I leaned up slightly, watching my hand move inside her, and it was driving me crazy.

I wanted nothing more than to jerk these slacks down my legs and fuck her until she couldn't remember anything but me.

"Do you know how many times I've thought about you?" I kissed the inside of her thigh, and she jumped. "How many times I've gotten myself off thinking about you making these exact same noises?"

"I'm going to come." She arched off the ground and slammed her eyes closed.

"Eyes back on me, baby."

She did as I said without hesitation, and when her gaze met mine, I slowly lowered back down and brought my mouth back to her pussy. I quickly moved my tongue over her clit, and she tightened her thighs around my head.

"You come when I say." I stared up at her and watched as her breath caught in her throat.

"Olly, I don't think I can—"

Her voice cut off as I sucked her clit hard into my mouth and curled my fingers over and over inside her. Her thighs shook and her mouth opened in a gasp, and it was the most beautiful sight I had ever seen.

"Come on my face, Frankie," I demanded of her. "Let me taste how badly you want me on my tongue."

She fell apart then, her pussy clamping down around my fingers and her thighs doing the same around my ears. She cried out loudly, without fear of who would hear us, and I didn't stop until I wrung every ounce of pleasure from her body.

When I finally rose to my knees, she was looking at me in a way that made my chest ache.

She fussed with her hair and sand fell from her long brown strands. "Do you still think I look decent enough to go to the after-party?"

I smiled and ran my tongue over my lips that still tasted like her. "You look fucking perfect." I leaned forward and kissed her, and if I didn't think the others would eventually come looking for us, I would have never moved from that spot.

CHAPTER 7
FRANKIE

"I feel like I could sleep for a week." Josie flopped over onto her back and groaned.

"If you didn't drink so much last night, you probably wouldn't feel that way."

She gave me the evilest look, and I laughed and held up my hands. "No judgment."

"It feels an awful lot like judgment." She chuckled and ran her hand over her forehead. "Where's Beck?"

"He went to get you something to eat." I nodded to her side table. "But he left you some water and ibuprofen over there."

I loved that she lived with us now even though I wished the circumstances weren't what they were. I never expected to be best friends with Lucas's stepsister, and I was sure she never expected to move in with her boyfriend's parents because her own father was horrid.

My parents had thought having her stay in the pool house versus the main house would keep some separation between her and Beck, but they were dead wrong. He had practically moved in out here too.

"Did I embarrass myself last night?" She reached out for the ibuprofen and groaned.

"If you'd be embarrassed by table dancing and proclaiming how much of a god Beck is in bed" —I gagged playfully— "then yes. Otherwise, you're good."

"Oh my God." She groaned loudly, and I laughed at the regret on her face.

"Take a shower and pull yourself together, then let's just hang at the pool today."

I was already in my suit, and even though I didn't drink nearly as much as Josie, I felt bone-tired myself. I knew it was from the two orgasms Olly had pulled from my body yesterday and the way my body still felt like it was on fire from his touch.

I had spent almost the entire party last night watching him, and he had been looking at me too. He had been staring at me like he wanted nothing more than to continue what we had been doing on the beach, and I wanted that as well. I craved it more than I had ever realized.

I had never experienced anything like that before. When he had laid me out in front of him, I had felt so self-conscious. It didn't matter how brave I acted or how badly I wanted him, that tug of doubt was always present in my mind.

He had always been present since what happened.

And part of me was worried that all he could think about when he looked at me was what Lucas had done.

I knew that wasn't rational. Olly had never once given me any reason to think that, but it still nagged at the back of my mind.

I had been so anxious about how I would feel, how I would react when he touched me, but he had eased those worries so effortlessly.

And I felt freer in a way I hadn't been since everything happened.

I barely remembered what happened with Lucas that night, but I was still haunted by the memory of it. Of what others told me. Of the flashes that still came through.

I had liked Lucas then, and he took advantage of that fact. I remembered how he whispered in my ear as he touched me. The words were foggy but the sound of his voice was clear. My eyes had been so heavy with alcohol, and even though I wanted him to stop, I couldn't remember if I had managed to say the words out loud.

That was the worst part. I didn't know if I had asked Lucas to touch me or if I had begged him to stop. All I knew was that I had been a fool, and everything had been different after what happened. Beck, Carson, and Olly all treated me differently. They had changed because I had changed and that made me feel even worse.

But what had happened with Olly last night? That made me feel different. That made me feel really and truly alive despite my fears, and I wouldn't be sorry for it.

"Is Allie here?" Josie walked into the bathroom but left the door open as she turned on the shower.

"She should be here any minute." I looked down at my phone to check the time and couldn't stop smiling when I saw a text from Olly.

Olly: Where are you?

Me: Pool house. Where are you?

"Okay. Good. We've been spending too much time with the guys lately. We need a girls' day."

"Agreed." I nodded, but I had barely heard a thing she said as I watched the three little dots bounce across my screen.

Olly: Waiting on you.

The next text was a photo of him in the pool, and God, he looked so damn handsome.

Me: Who said I was going swimming?

I chewed on my bottom lip as I waited for his reply.

Olly: Well, I can see you sitting in there in that tiny pink bikini, and I've been thinking about you all night. I could still taste you on my tongue as I got myself off last night. If you're not coming swimming, then I'm coming in after you.

My gaze snapped up to the set of glass French doors that separated the pool house from the pool area, and sure enough, Olly was leaning against the pool edge with his head resting on his arms and his eyes staring directly at me.

I swallowed hard and gripped my phone in my hand.

"I'm going to head out to the pool!" I yelled out to Josie, and she replied with a quick okay.

I gathered my towel and phone in my hand and slid my sunglasses onto my face as I walked outside. Olly was the only one there, and I closed the glass door behind me before leaning against it and staring back at him.

"Well, aren't you a sight for sore eyes?" He grinned, and I watched as water trickled from his dark hair down his shoulders. His gaze ran over my body so slowly that it would have felt indecent if anyone else was around.

"We're supposed to be having a girls' day." As soon as I said the words, his grin became bigger, and he cocked his head to the side.

"Are you saying that you don't want me?"

"No." I quickly shook my head because we both knew that was the furthest thing from the truth. "I'm just saying the girls might not be so happy about you being here."

I pushed off the door and made my way toward him. I dropped my towel and phone down on the nearest chair, and I didn't stop until I sat down beside him and dipped my toes in the pool.

"Do you really think either one of them is going to spend any significant amount of time without Beck or Carson?" He shook his head before his arm pressed against my leg, and he turned toward me.

"Probably not." I shrugged and splashed my feet through the water.

"Plus, they love me."

I cocked my head to the side and watched him. "I didn't realize how cocky you were until recently." Cocky and demanding and capable of making my stomach tighten by just looking at him.

"I'm not cocky." He cupped some water in his hand before letting it fall over my knee. The sun was blaring down on my back, but a cold chill ran through me. He traced a finger over my skin following the movement of the water. "I'm just sure when it comes to certain things."

"Like?" I asked, then regretted it instantly. I wanted him to say me, but I knew that wasn't what he meant. He could be sure of this and that still wouldn't mean me.

"Like..." He moved even closer to me, and his abs pressed against my shins. "The fact that I don't care whether the girls want me here or not. I'm staying."

I opened my mouth to speak, but he wasn't done.

"I'm also sure about the fact that you are driving me fucking crazy." His hand trailed under the water, and he gripped my ankle in his palm. He ran fingers up and down my calf, and I tightened my thighs.

"I'm not doing anything."

"The fuck you aren't." He chuckled, and his gaze ran over every inch of me. "I've never wanted someone so fucking badly in all my life."

I looked up toward the house as his words ran over me like a caress, but I still saw no signs of the others.

I pushed my thighs open a few inches and his gaze instantly dropped between them.

"Your brother is going to be back soon," he spoke without ever looking up.

"I know." I nodded even though I could barely catch my breath under his gaze. "Josie's probably getting out of the shower right now too."

"Right." Both of his hands were moving up and down my calves now, and I could feel his fingers tighten against me as he spoke.

"I want to touch you," I whispered with what little bravery I had, and his gaze snapped up to mine.

"That's not going to happen. Not here."

"Why not?" I lifted myself off the side of the pool and slowly sank into the water in front of him. My body slid against his as I fell into the water, and I wrapped my legs around his waist before leaning back against the pool wall.

"You're dangerous, Frankie," Olly whispered before looking down where our bodies met.

"No. I'm not." I shook my head and rolled my hips. "I'm turned on." *And you make me feel like that isn't a sin.*

"Fuck," he cursed under his breath before looking back over his shoulder. I knew what he was looking for. I knew he was worried we'd be caught, but I couldn't bring myself to care at that moment. I just wanted him to touch me. I would do anything for him to.

"Do you not want me?" I moved my hips again, and he groaned low and deep.

"You know I want you, Frankie, but we can't do this here."

"I'm not asking you to fuck me. I just want to feel you."

His hands moved to my hips, and they were so tight that I felt the edge of pain. I could see the hesitation in his eyes, and I didn't want him to say no. I was desperate for him not to say no.

"I've never touched anyone else before." I searched his eyes as I spoke. "I don't think." Flashes of what happened with Lucas flickered in my mind, and I tried to force them away.

I didn't know if Olly could see the shift in my face or the doubt in my eyes, but either way, his hands tightened around me, and he pulled me closer to him. "I am desperate for you to touch me," he growled out the words. "But I don't want you to do anything you're not ready for."

My hand shook as I lowered it between us and pressed it against his trunks. He was hard against me, and I gasped as I felt him. He was so much bigger than I expected, and I had no idea what I was doing.

"I'm ready." My voice shook, betraying my words. "I want to make you feel like you made me. I want you to feel good."

"You do." He searched my face before looking back down between us. "God, Frankie. You make me feel everything."

"Then let me do this," I begged of him. I knew that he had probably done far more with lots of other girls, but it didn't matter. I needed this. I needed to touch him and know that he was as wrapped up in my every move as I was in his.

He stared into my eyes as I ran my hand over his stomach. His muscles rippled beneath my touch, and I tried to stop the trembling of my fingers.

As safe as he made me feel, I was still nervous. I was so damn scared of fucking this up.

I slid my hand beneath the band of his trunks, and he hissed as my skin met his. I was hesitant as I wrapped my hand around him, and I didn't move for a second as I took in the feel of him.

His skin was so soft, and I felt mesmerized as I finally moved and explored the length of him.

"Fuck," he groaned and jerked my hips forward until my pussy was pressed against my hand and him.

I tightened my legs around him, and I ground my hips down against my hand.

"God, you feel so good." He leaned forward, and my breath caught in my throat as his ragged breath pushed in and out against my neck. He pressed a gentle kiss there, and I felt it as if he had done it directly between my thighs.

"I want you in…"

"Is Beck not back yet with food?" We jerked apart at the sound of Josie's voice, and I almost plunged into the water as I dropped to my feet.

I could barely catch my breath, let alone answer her.

"Not yet." Olly looked up at her before running his wet hands through his hair. "I think he might have gotten lost."

"Agreed." Josie threw her towel down on the chair beside mine before pulling her hair back in a bun. "But your girl needs some food in her stomach."

Olly was looking at me as she spoke, and I couldn't look away. I pressed my thighs together to try to stop the ache that felt like it was burning inside me, but it did nothing to help.

"Yeah." Olly sank down until the water was above his shoulders. "You put on quite the show last night. I figured you'd still be in bed."

"I would be." Josie rested her hand against her temple as she made her way into the pool. "But your girl over there woke me up."

Hearing her call me his girl fucked with my head, and I was already too far gone to be thinking clearly.

I let myself fall under the water, and I tried to clear my head as the water surrounded me. I didn't know what the hell I was thinking. Anyone could have just seen us. Hell, if Josie wasn't hungover, grouchy, and not paying attention, she would have seen exactly what we were doing.

We got lucky because if that had been Beck, we'd be dead.

I rose back out of the water, and Olly's eyes were still on me. He was watching me carefully, looking for what I was thinking or feeling, but I just smiled and looked over at my friend.

"You're grouchy when you're hungover."

"No shit." She laughed and sighed as she sank into the water. "I'm hungry, I have a headache, and I'm sex-deprived."

Mine and Olly's gazes snapped to one another.

"Beck not taking care of your needs?" Olly chuckled, and Josie rolled her eyes.

"He more than takes care of my needs, but I'm pretty sure I was a little too drunk last night and he was gone when I woke up this morning."

"God gave you fingers for a reason." I wiggled my hand out of the water, and she laughed.

"Not the same."

The back door to the house opened a second later, and

Beck pushed through, followed by Carson and Allie. His arms were full of bags of tacos, and he searched out Josie as soon as he made it outside.

"She's alive!" he cheered with a chuckle.

"No thanks to you." She leaned back in the water and let it saturate her hair. "You left me."

I rolled my eyes playfully at the pout on her face, but it dropped as soon as my brother leaned down on the side of the pool and pressed a kiss to her lips.

I felt Olly move behind me in the pool, and I looked over my shoulder at him. His fingers tangled with mine under the water, and he gave them a light squeeze.

"These fingers," he said so low that no one else could hear him. "Don't go near *my* pussy unless I'm there to watch."

I clamped my legs together and tried not to let him see how much his words affected me. "What?"

"You heard me." He moved past me, and I focused on fighting the urge to march straight up to my room and do exactly what he had just forbidden me to do.

I could barely pay attention as he climbed out of the pool and clapped hands with Carson then Beck. They all three laughed about something before Olly looked back in my direction.

I didn't know how to navigate this. More than anything, I wanted him to climb back into this pool and wrap me in his arms. Right here in front of everyone, but I knew that wasn't what we had agreed to.

And this reality was exactly what I told him I wanted.

"Did you get tacos for everyone?" Olly ran his hand down his abs, and I couldn't stop watching. "I'm fucking starving."

"Of course." Beck tossed him one of the bags, and Olly sat down in the seat with my things.

He pulled a taco out of the bag, and I swear to God, he was staring me straight in my eyes as he took his first bite.

Why in the hell did he look so hot doing that?

"Frankie, you want some?" He held out the taco in my direction even though he was no longer anywhere near me.

"Yeah." I stood on shaking legs and pushed my hair out of my face. No one but him was paying a bit of attention to me, but I felt like I had a neon light flashing across my chest that told them how freaking turned on I was.

I made my way toward him and leaned over him to grab my towel. Water dropped off my body onto his, and I smirked at the way he was staring at me.

I wiped my hands off on my towel before dropping it into his lap and grabbing the taco out of his hand. He chuckled as I took a huge bite of the taco and closed my eyes as the taste hit me.

It was absolutely delicious.

I swallowed and took another bite, finishing off the taco.

"That was my taco, you know?" He squinted as he stared up at me and the sun hit his eyes.

"You offered it." I shrugged and wiped my mouth with my hand.

"I did." He wrapped his hand around the back of my knee and tugged me toward him. My gaze shot up to look at everyone else, but they weren't paying us any bit of attention. "But I figured you would at least share it with me."

"I'm not much for sharing."

"I can see that." His finger made small circles on the back of my knee, and how in the hell did that simple touch feel so obscene? "Who knew you were so greedy."

"Olly," I whispered his name in warning because he was playing a game, and I knew that I was going to lose. I was standing here in front of him and all of our friends, and I was so turned on that I should have been embarrassed.

"What do you need, Frankie?" He cocked his head to the side with the most handsome smirk on his face.

"Nothing." I took a step back from him, and his fingers fell from my leg. "I just need to run in the house and take care of something really quickly."

He narrowed his eyes at me, and I returned his smirk from only a second before.

"You wouldn't dare."

"Wouldn't I?" I turned from him before I talked myself out of it. "I'm going to go grab some floats," I said the first thing I could think of, and when no one questioned me, I headed into the house.

I climbed up the stairs as quickly as my feet would carry me and leaned against my bedroom door as I closed it.

Olly wasn't playing fair, and I felt like I was going out of my mind. My heart was pounding in my chest, and when I closed my eyes, all I could see was the way he had been looking at me.

My bathing suit was still wet, and it was rubbing against my skin. I took a deep breath before pushing off my door and walking into the bathroom. I needed to get my shit together before I did something stupid.

I turned on the shower before pressing my hands against the counter and staring in the mirror.

My cheeks were flushed from the sun and my nerves, and my eyes looked glazed over with lust. I pulled at the ties of my bikini top before letting it fall to the floor, then I shimmied out of my bottoms.

I climbed into the shower, and I sighed when the hot water hit my skin.

I leaned my head back and let the water flow over me, and I tried to calm my racing heart. But all I could think about was him.

I ran my fingers over my hair before pressing them into my neck. Every inch of my skin felt like it was burning with need, and despite what Olly said, I couldn't wait for the next time the two of us would get to be together.

Heck, I had no idea when that would even be.

I slid my hands down my chest until they reached my breasts and squeezed them gently. I was so turned on that I could already feel the moisture between my legs. I was pretty sure it hadn't left since my hand had been on Olly in the pool.

I pushed my right hand down my stomach and took a steadying breath. This was something that I could control. My hand and my need were more than familiar with each other, and other than Olly, I was the only person that had ever brought me to orgasm.

The water cascaded down my body, racing my hand to its destination, and I leaned my shoulders back against the shower wall as I let my eyes flutter closed.

"Didn't I tell you not to let those fingers touch my pussy?"

I jumped and my gaze snapped open at the sound of Olly's voice, and I almost slipped at the panic of seeing him leaning against my bathroom vanity.

"What are you doing in here?" I crossed my arms over my chest, and he cocked an eyebrow.

"You ran off. I wanted to make sure you were okay. Plus, you were taking an awful long time to get a pool float, and you went in the wrong direction."

"I'm fine." I ground out and pressed my thighs together. The ache that was there was starting to throb and watching him stare at me was only making it worse. "I just needed to take a shower."

"Something wrong?" His lips lifted in an almost smile, and I wanted to throw myself at him.

"Yeah." I nodded and decided that lying to him was useless. "You got me all worked up, and I feel like I'm dying." I pushed my fingers through my folds despite his warning not to.

"Frankie." His voice was commanding, but it had the opposite effect of what he wanted it to have. Instead of making me stop, it only spurred me on harder.

"Yes, Olly?" I asked him and tilted my head to the side as I leaned back against the shower wall and circled my clit with my finger.

His gaze was glued to my hand through the glass shower door, and it felt like he was physically touching me.

He pushed off my vanity, and my chest ached as he walked toward the door. The urge to call out his name and beg him not to leave was overwhelming, but as soon as the thought crossed my mind, his fingers twisted the lock on my bathroom door.

He turned back to face me, and the look in his eyes was so territorial, it was almost enough to push me over the edge.

"Are you coming in?" I asked him as I began moving my hand in small circles.

"No." He shook his head before making his way back to my vanity and lifting himself until he was sitting atop it.

"I'm going to watch." He laid his hand against his bare stomach, and the sight fueled me on.

He was so damn handsome, and he was looking at me like he wanted to devour me.

"I don't want you to watch." I lifted my other hand and pushed my wet hair out of my face. "I want you to touch me."

"You should have thought about that before you came up here and decided to do this without me." He grinned and ran his hand over the front of his swimming trunks. "Now I get to see exactly what you were disobeying me for."

"I didn't realize I was supposed to be obeying you." I stared at him, but even as I said the words, I knew that what he said sent a thrill through me. I wanted to give Olly any and every single thing that he wanted.

"Well, now you know." He stared down between my legs. "Now open your legs wider so I can see you better."

I immediately obeyed his request, and the curve of his lips quirked up higher.

"Good girl."

I moaned as my finger slid over my clit, and I let my eyes fall closed as I leaned my head back.

"Look at me, Frankie." His voice was commanding, and I snapped my eyes open just as his hands were untying his shorts. "Keep your eyes on me."

Even if he hadn't told me to, I wouldn't have been able to look away. He pulled his cock out of his shorts, and he hissed as his hand ran over it from tip to base.

I wanted to do that. I wanted to be the one to make him hiss and moan and beg for more.

I pushed off the shower wall and reached for the door, but Olly stopped me.

"You come out of the shower, and this stops." His hand was moving up and down his cock slowly and firmly, and I felt desperate to replace his hand with mine.

"Olly," I called out his name, and he shook his head.

"No. Get back against that wall and show me exactly what you do to your pussy." He squeezed the tip of his cock, and I watched as moisture beaded there. "Show me how you touch yourself when you think of me."

I did as he said, falling back against the wall and spreading myself open with my fingers. I ran my middle finger over my clit while I watched him, and I knew I needed more.

"Am I the only one you think about when your hand is buried in your pussy?"

"Yes." My answer was immediate, and I pushed my finger inside myself while using my other hand to roll my nipple. "It's always you."

"Tell me what you think about." He groaned, and I watched as his hand sped up.

"It depends." I began pumping my hand in and out of my pussy and pushed my palm down hard against my clit. "Sometimes I imagine you coming to my room in the middle of the night when everyone is asleep."

His eyes burned as they stared into mine. "And what do I do once I'm in here?"

"You climb into my bed and clamp your hand over my mouth so I don't scream and wake everyone up." I slid my finger back up and spread the moisture over my clit. Olly was watching my every move, and it felt like a drug.

"Where do I touch you? Where's my mouth?"

"Everywhere." I was barely able to breathe out the word as my legs began to tremble. "You keep your hand on my mouth as you work your way down my body, and you don't leave an inch untouched." I bit down on my lip. "Olly, I'm going to come."

"Not yet." His command shot out and his hand moved faster against his cock. "Do I fuck you in these fantasies of yours?"

"Yes." I moaned and braced one of my hands against the wall. "Every time. You... oh God... you..."

"Let me tell you what I would do," he growled, and I couldn't look away from him.

"I would fuck you until my cum was running down your legs and you could still feel my hand on your throat after I walked away."

"Olly," I moaned his name and pressed my legs together to try to keep myself from coming. It was no use. I was so far on the edge that there was nothing that was going to stop the rush that was racing through me.

"Open your fucking legs, Frankie."

I did as he said and moaned even louder. I was praying that Beck and everyone else was still out at the pool, but in reality, I couldn't bring myself to care. Beck could be banging on the bathroom door, and I still wouldn't be able to stop.

"When I fuck you, I'm going to make sure that I ruin you for anyone else who comes after me. You're mine, Frankie, and you're going to know it."

"I am yours," I whimpered and his hand jerked harshly against his cock.

"Come."

That one word snapped something inside of me, and I came with a scream. I covered my mouth with my hand, but it was torn off and replaced with Olly's mouth. His hands tangled in my hair and tugged at the base of my skull as he jerked me closer to him.

He kissed me like he was drowning and I was his only source of air. Our stomachs were pressed together, and I could feel the evidence of his own orgasm as it coated my skin.

He leaned back and stared down at me, his hands still holding me in place, and I could barely catch my breath as I looked up at him.

"I should get back down to the pool before they miss me."

I nodded. "You should."

He searched my eyes but didn't move. I felt like he was warring with himself over whether or not to leave me, and I knew it would be selfish of me to ask him to stay.

He dropped his gaze down to where we met before looking back up at me. "Let me clean you up first."

He didn't wait for my answer. He simply grabbed my loofah and squirted a bit of body wash on it before lathering it up.

He slowly ran the loofah over my neck before dropping it down to my breasts and washing the sensitive skin there. His eyes looked so dark as he watched what he was doing, and he ran his tongue over his lip as he moved to my stomach.

"I love seeing my cum on you," he moaned, and despite the warm water that was still flowing, chill bumps coated my skin.

He moved the loofah even lower and slid it along my pussy with the most gentle touch. "I'm fucking dying to see it here." He pressed the loofah harder against me and ran it up and down my center.

I trembled and reached forward, gripping his biceps in my hands. I stared down at where he was touching me with the loofah, and I could already feel another orgasm building inside me.

"I thought you needed to leave."

"I do," he grumbled, and a deep crease formed on his forehead just between his eyes. The loofah fell from his hand, and I gasped as his finger slid against my clit. "But I can't leave this fucking room until I make you come again. I want to show you how much better it can be with me."

He walked forward until I was forced to lean back against the wall, and he kissed me hard as his fingers started moving against me. His other hand tangled back in my hair, and he tugged on the strands until I was forced to look straight up at him.

He bit down on my lower lip to the point of pain just as he slid a finger inside me. I moaned, and he licked the spot he had just bitten before moving down my chin.

His mouth bombarded me with a combination of his soft, lethal tongue and his teeth that had me squirming, and his hand was no different. He pumped his finger harshly inside me before slowing down again and touching a spot inside me that had me clinging to him to stay upright.

He lowered his head to my nipple and caressed the small bud with his tongue before pulling it into his mouth. He pulled his hand from my pussy, and I trembled as he ran it back over my stomach. His fingers moved just below my belly button and swirled in the soap and his cum that still remained on my skin.

"I can't fucking wait." He lifted his fingers from me, and I could see his cum coating the tips of his fingers. He lowered his hand back down my body, and I had to hold on to him for support when his fingers spread me open and spread his cum against my clit.

"Oh God."

My orgasm raced through me quickly, and I knew this one was going to hit me so much harder than the one before.

I was still so sensitive from only moments earlier and watching him cover me in him made me feel powerless against him.

Olly dropped to his knees in front of me as he continued working his hand, and he stared straight ahead and watched everything he was doing to me.

"Whose pussy is this?"

"What?" I squeaked and tried to catch my breath. I was so close to coming, and I could barely think, let alone answer his questions.

"You heard me, Frankie. Whose pussy is this?" he growled.

"It's yours."

As soon as I gave him his answer, he leaned forward and sucked my clit into his mouth. It was sudden and overwhelming, and his fingers pushed back inside me without faltering.

"Oh fuck." I grabbed a hold of his shoulders as I was hit with the force of my orgasm.

He gripped my thighs in his hands and held me upright against the wall.

I slammed my eyes shut as he continued to work every ounce of pleasure from my body. Every inch of my skin felt like it was buzzing, and I took deep breaths over and over as I tried to bring myself down from the high he had given me.

I had never come so hard in my entire life.

"I really need to go now." He was still on his knees in front of me, and he leaned forward and pressed a gentle kiss to my pussy before standing.

"Yeah." I nodded frantically, but it was the only amount of movement I could manage. My legs felt so weak that I was sure I would fall if I attempted to walk.

He kissed me again, this time gentler than all the rest, and I could taste myself on his lips along with traces of something else that I knew was him. He opened the door to the shower and quickly dried himself off with one of my towels before he looked back at me.

His eyes were still glazed over in lust, and it was impossible to miss how hard he still was.

"I have to go."

I couldn't help but laugh. "So you've said."

His gaze snapped back up to meet mine, and he smiled. He pushed his hair back out of his face before hanging my towel back on its hook. He tucked his cock back into his shorts before tying the small string.

"You're going to be so much fucking trouble."

I finally pushed off the wall and took a small step before turning off the water. Olly handed me a towel, and I began running it over my arms. "Why is that?"

"Because." He was watching me, and his gaze roamed back over my body as if he was battling with himself to walk away. "I want to fuck you so badly that I can't seem to remember the consequences."

"Consequences are overrated," I murmured, and wrapped the towel around my body that was still electrified from his touch.

"I think they might be." His gaze lingered on me one more time before he opened my bathroom door and disappeared from my space like he was never even there.

CHAPTER 8
OLLY

"Where are you going?"

I tucked my cell phone into my pocket and looked up at my father. "Out."

"Out where?" He set his glass down in front of him on the counter, and I noted the dark liquor that filled it. He seemed to always have it these days.

"With my friends." I crossed my arms and looked around for my mom, but I didn't see her anywhere. "What's with the fifth degree?"

"Asking my son where he's going is not the fifth degree."

"From you it is." Unease filled me because he never cared where I was or what the hell I was doing. Why the fuck did he suddenly care now?

My father chuckled and swirled the liquor in his glass. "Once upon a time, I knew everything about you. Remember that?"

"Yeah." I nodded and looked away from him. Of course, I remembered that, but my father and I hadn't been like that in years. I grew up, and he got busy.

He was always busy.

"So, what's going on with you and Beck's sister?"

"She has a name." My voice was much harsher than I meant it to be, but I couldn't stand that he was talking about her.

"Calm down." He chuckled and held up his hand. "I know she has a name. What's going on with you and Frankie?"

"There's nothing going on." I clenched my fist and tried not to let him see any reaction from me.

He rubbed his jaw as he studied me. "I may not know everything, but boy, only a fool would believe that lie."

I didn't know what to say, so I told him the one thing that I had been repeating to myself over the years. "She's Beck's sister."

"I'm aware." He nodded his head. "You're young, Olly. There will be hundreds of Frankies in the next few years. That girl isn't worth ruining your friendship with Beck over."

My jaw felt like it was going to snap as I thought about what he just said. I knew that he was just trying to talk some sense into me. Sense that I tried talking into myself, but he didn't fucking understand. He didn't know Frankie the way I did. "You don't even know her."

"I don't need to."

He was so fucking wrong.

Everything felt wrong. Everything but her, and I knew that wasn't logical. But even though she was the one thing I wasn't supposed to want, she was the one thing I felt was effortless.

"Don't fuck up things with the Clermonts because you're thinking with your dick instead of your head." He chuckled, but I heard the tone behind it. That was his specialty, being a dick without everyone else seeing it.

I bit my tongue as I listened to his ignorance. He only saw people for what they could do for him. He didn't give a shit that Beck was my best friend. He only cared that his father was wealthy and influential.

"I have to go." I laughed without an ounce of humor because I couldn't stand to listen to another word from him. "Don't worry. I'll make sure not to make any decisions with my dick tonight."

I was almost to the door when his next words hit me. "Just don't be an idiot, Olly."

I let the door thud behind me and sent Frankie a text as I climbed into my car. I didn't care what he said. I needed to see her.

Let's do something.

I was halfway to her house when her reply came in.

Frankie: Okay. Like what?

It doesn't matter. Meet me outside in 5.

I felt like an asshole because I desperately wanted to go in and get her. I wanted to knock on her fucking door and let everyone know that she was coming with me, but I couldn't.

If I went in there, Beck would think I was here for him. There would be too many questions about why I wanted to leave with Frankie.

So instead, I pulled up outside her house, and I smiled for the first time tonight when I spotted her leaning against the house wearing a pair of cutoff blue jean shorts, a white tank top, and a pair of old Vans.

She was so effortlessly beautiful, and it drove me fucking crazy. Her hair had the slightest wave to it like it did once it dried from the ocean, and her face didn't have an ounce of makeup on it.

I climbed out of the car as she headed in my direction with a soft smile on her full pink lips, and I stared at her over the hood.

"Did you already have plans?"

"No." She shook her head and looked at me curiously. "Why?"

"Because I just text you and you walk out of your house looking like that." I waved my hand in her direction, and my gaze caught on the deep tan of her perfect fucking thighs.

"You're insane, Olly." She rolled her eyes as I moved toward the car.

"I'm not." I opened the passenger side door, then leaned back against it. "Tell me if I need to kick someone's ass."

"What if I did have plans?" She stepped in front of me, and the slightest hint of coconut hit me. "Maybe I should text him back and let him know I'm still available."

"Sure." I crowded her space and blocked her from climbing in my car. "If you'd like to see me be a jealous asshole tonight."

"I bet you're so hot when you're jealous."

"You've seen me jealous a million times before." I pushed some hair behind her ear before running my finger along her jaw.

"No. I haven't."

"Yes. You have." My thumb trailed over her bottom lip. "I've been jealous of anyone who's touched you or talked to you or been close to you for years."

I lifted her hand in mine and pressed a small kiss against her fingertips. "I've been jealous of these perfect fucking fingers and the thought that they get to touch you when I'm not able to."

Frankie's chest rose and fell and her gaze fell to my lips. "We're still in my driveway," she whispered, and it should have knocked some sense into me.

But it didn't.

I was so damn distracted by her that I couldn't bring myself to care about anything else.

"We should go." I leaned closer to her, and the urge to kiss her was overwhelming.

"We really should." She put her hand against my chest and forced me to stop only inches from her. "Now get me out of here."

She squeezed past me, her body sliding against mine, and I felt like she had just stripped me bare. She had barely even touched me, and already all I could think about was getting her beneath me.

I climbed into the driver's side of my car, and I tried to focus on anything other than her as I started the engine and pulled out of her driveway.

"Where are we going exactly?"

"I really hadn't thought that part through." I chuckled and ran my fingers through my hair. I made the mistake of looking over at her, and God, she was so beautiful. I laid my hand against her thigh, just above her knee, and I pressed my fingers into her soft skin. "I just wanted to be alone with you for a little while."

"Okay." She smiled, and I could have sworn she shifted and her thighs separated by the smallest amount. "I'm up for anything."

"I've got an idea." I made a sharp turn to head in the direction I was thinking, and Frankie laughed.

"That doesn't make me nervous at all."

"Trust me." I grinned at her.

"I do." She nodded, and I felt those words in my gut.

I drove us away from the coast for about thirty minutes, and Frankie never questioned me once. She trusted me, and protecting her trust felt like the most important thing I could imagine.

She sat up in her seat and her eyes lit up as we pulled up next to the old boat rental shop next to the lake.

"Are we getting a boat?" She practically squealed, and I couldn't help laughing because her excitement was so contagious.

The sun was already starting to set, and I was honestly surprised this place was still open.

"If you want to." I turned off the car and looked out my windshield. There was one small boat parked on the water, but I didn't see any others in sight. "We can at least try."

"Oh my God." Frankie unbuckled her seat belt and flung her door open. "I'm so excited."

I climbed out of the car and jogged around it to catch up to her. Her hand fit so perfectly in mine as I grabbed hold of it, and I couldn't help but smile as I watched her look down at our hands like we were doing something wrong.

No one was here to see us, to tell us that we weren't supposed to be doing this.

"Let's go see what they have."

We pushed through the door, and a loud bell rang, alerting them we were here.

"One sec!" a voice called from somewhere in the back, and Frankie leaned into me as we waited.

I kissed the top of her forehead, and she looked up at me with her nose scrunched. "This feels weird."

"What?" I chuckled and ran my finger down her nose.

"This." She bumped her shoulder against me. "It's a good weird, though."

"It is." I gripped her chin in my hand and tilted her face until she was at the perfect angle. "I like that I don't have to hide this." I leaned down and caught her mouth against mine. She melted against me, her body leaning into me for support, and I gave it to her. I would give her anything she wanted at this point.

"How can I help you two?"

Frankie jerked away from me at the sound of the old man's voice, but I kept my arm wrapped around her.

"We were hoping it isn't too late to rent a boat for the evening."

He rubbed his hand over his chin as he looked us over. "Either of you twenty-five years old?"

I winced at his question. I hadn't even thought about that. "No. I'm eighteen."

"Well, son. The best I can do for you is an old canoe I have around the back."

"We'll take it," Frankie answered before I could. I stared over at her because what in the hell were we going to do with a canoe? But the smile on her face was contagious, and there was no chance of me telling her no.

I sighed and pulled my wallet out of my back pocket, but the old man shook his head. "I got no need for your money. The damn thing is so old it might just sink on y'all out there."

"That sounds promising."

"Take it or leave it." He shrugged his shoulders.

"We want it. Thank you." Frankie smacked my arm as

she bounced on her feet. She didn't care if we sank to the bottom of the lake. She was excited either way.

"Follow me." He waved for us, and we followed him out of the back of the building.

As soon as we stepped outside, I spotted the rusting canoe leaning against a tree near the water. I shook my head as soon as I saw it, but Frankie tugged on my hand and pulled me further.

"There are oars over there." He pointed them out. "I may be closed by the time the two of you get done, but just put it back when you're finished."

"We will. Thank you again." Frankie was still pulling me down to the canoe, and I gave her a look that should have told her that there was no way in hell we were doing this.

But Frankie just tapped her fingers against the base of the canoe and grinned at me.

"Do you think you can carry this or should I ask the old man to help you?" She bit her lip to stop from laughing, and God, she looked so happy.

"I've got it, but do not blame me when we sink to the bottom."

She shrugged her shoulders. "I can swim."

"Okay, smartass." I lifted the canoe from the tree as Frankie grabbed the two oars. "Get your ass down to the water."

She walked in front of me, and the sway of her hips was so damn mesmerizing that I almost tripped over a tree root. I cursed under my breath, and Frankie looked back at me with a smirk.

"Are you okay back there?"

"I'm fine. You're just distracting."

She stopped at the edge of the water and cocked her eyebrow. "How am I distracting? All I did was walk."

"That's all it took."

I pushed the canoe off my shoulder and set it at the edge of the lake. It was a lot heavier than it looked, but there was no way I was admitting that to Frankie. I pushed it into the water until only one end was still on shore.

"Ladies first." I grabbed the oars from her and set them down inside the canoe. I reached my hand out for Frankie, and she took it as she stepped into the small boat. It rocked as she climbed in, and I laughed as she squealed and clung onto the sides.

She dropped into the seat and held on to the sides for dear life as I pushed us off the bank and jumped inside.

"You're going to flip us!" She grabbed an oar against her chest, and I had no idea what she planned on doing with it.

"You said you know how to swim."

"That doesn't mean I want to." She looked down at the green water that was so different than the ocean she was used to swimming in. "I don't even know what's in there."

"You swim in the ocean all the time, and trust me, there are far scarier things in there." I grabbed the other oar and pressed the end into the smooth water. I slipped it into the oar socket before reaching out and grabbing the other from Frankie.

Once I had them both in place, I pushed them both into the water and propelled us forward.

"How do you know how to do this?" Frankie pointed at the oars, and I laughed.

"It's not rocket science, Frankie. Don't look so impressed."

"I'm always impressed by you." She shrugged like that simple statement was no big deal.

But it was, and it was enough to make me want to open up to her about things I didn't talk to anyone about. Things I hated thinking about.

"My dad used to bring me out here." I looked around at the lake, and I could have sworn the smell of the trees was locked away in my memories. "We would do just about anything you can think of, including rowing in old canoes."

"I didn't know that." She looked at me with a look I couldn't decipher, and I hated that.

"It was a long time ago. Before I became friends with Beck."

"Do you miss doing things like this?"

"Of course." I nodded my head and my chest felt tight. "But if my dad tried to bring me out here now, it would be fucking awkward. We wouldn't have a single thing to talk about."

"I feel like your dad doesn't understand you."

"He doesn't." I shook my head and tried to shake off the feelings that were bombarding me. "His and my mom's lives revolve around work and money. I guess it has always been that way, but it didn't use to feel like that. But now, I swear that's all they think about."

"And they don't want you to play baseball anymore?"

"My dad doesn't want me to leave." I clenched the oars in my hands as I thought about the countless conversations I've had with my parents on this very subject. "He thinks that I'm going to waste years of my life playing college baseball when I should just be getting a business degree here and working for him at the same time."

"But you're still getting a business degree, right?"

"I am, but he doesn't care. That's not good enough for him."

"What do your parents actually do anyway?" She was watching me so intently, but I honestly just wanted to change the subject. I didn't bring her out here to talk about my parents. I brought her out here because I just wanted to be alone with her for a second without worrying who was seeing us.

"They own an investment company. It's honestly the most boring thing I can imagine doing with my life."

"Then don't do it." Frankie shrugged and leaned down to run her fingers through the water. We were so far from the bank at this point that I could barely see my car.

"It's not that easy."

"Life isn't meant to be easy." Her dark eyes looked up at me, and I felt like she could see past every one of my defenses. "So, do whatever you want."

I let go of the oars and scooted up in my seat until my knees hit hers. "Right now, the only thing I want is you."

"You have me," she whispered, and I knew that she meant it. She meant it more than I deserved, but I refused to let her take any of it back. I was meant to be this safe place for her, but instead, I was keeping her a secret. I made her a lie instead of facing her brother, and I hated myself for it.

"What do you want?"

She bit her bottom lip as she contemplated my question. "I don't know."

"Yes. You do."

Her hand moved into her hair, and I could tell she was so unsure of herself. But I gave her time. "I just don't want to be this girl." She motioned up and down her body.

"What do you mean?" I loved this girl.

A deep crease formed between her brows. "I mean that I don't want everyone to look at me and see the girl who was assaulted. I want to feel free. To not have anyone look at me and think about Lucas."

My heart hammered in my chest at her words. "I don't see him when I look at you."

"Yes. You do." She nodded. "That's why you all think I'm so damn breakable. You all see me as so damn fragile, but I'm not."

I moved forward another inch, and the canoe rocked as I wrapped my hand around her jaw.

"Olly!" She reached out and clung to the sides, but I didn't give a fuck if this damn thing flipped. I felt like I was going to die if I didn't kiss her.

"What?" I murmured against her lips before tracing her bottom one with my tongue. "Do you want me to stop?"

She shook her head, and I could feel her rushed breath against my mouth.

"You are not fragile, Frankie. You are fire. Uncontrollable and strong. You don't have a fucking clue how I see you."

She didn't hesitate. She closed the space between us without another thought, and I moaned as I tasted her for the first time in what felt like days. Her tongue caressed mine gently before I tightened my hand on her jaw and kissed her harder.

Her hands moved to my chest, and I could feel her fingertips digging into me as she grasped my shirt. My knee pressed between hers, and I bit down on her bottom lip. She whimpered and the sound went straight to my cock.

I ran my hand over her thigh, trailing it back and forth, and feeling the goose bumps that formed under my touch.

"You're so damn soft." My fingers dug in harder, and she separated her thighs the smallest bit.

"Uh-huh." She attempted to pull me closer to her, and she kissed me like she was just as turned on as I was. She clung to me, and I was unprepared when she pushed off her seat and straddled me in mine.

The canoe rocked hard to the left and water splashed into the boat as I jerked us back to the right.

"Oh my God." Frankie laughed and tried to climb out of my lap, but I held on to her. "We're going to tip!"

"You're the one who climbed on top of me." I chuckled and attempted to steady us.

"That's because you were rubbing my thigh and kissing me like that. So, technically, it's your fault." She stared down at me with the biggest smile on her face.

I pushed some of her dark hair out of her eyes before gripping her thighs and pulling her harder against me. "Fine. I'll take the blame."

"That was too easy." She ran her fingers through my hair and searched my face.

"I'll tell you whatever you need to hear for you to stay exactly where you are."

"Are you saying that you'd lie to me, Olly Warner?" She leaned back to get a better look at me, and the sun radiated around her as it finally sunk to the edge of the water.

"I'd like to do a lot worse to you."

She bit down on her bottom lip and her hands tightened in my hair. She pushed up slightly on her knees before her hips rolled gently against mine.

"I want you to do anything you want." She hadn't stopped moving her hips, and I couldn't stop staring up at her. "I would let you do anything."

"You're killing me, Frankie." I grabbed her hips in my hands to halt her movement, but she didn't care. She rolled her hips against me as if she couldn't feel me trying to stop her, as if she couldn't tell that it was taking everything inside me not to lose fucking control.

"I don't care." She shook her head. "I need you."

I clamped my eyes shut because I couldn't think clearly when she said that. There was nothing in the world that turned me on more, and I couldn't remember why I shouldn't lay her out on her back and fuck her right here on this damn half-broken-down boat.

"We're in the middle of the lake, Frankie." I leaned forward and ran my nose over her neck. She smelled so fucking good.

"Then take me somewhere else." She tugged on my hair to the point of pain and forced me to look up at her. "Take me somewhere and fuck me."

"Fuck." This wasn't my plan when I brought her out here, and now I felt like I couldn't think clearly. Frankie deserved far better than this, but I couldn't walk away.

I reached around her for the oars and dug them into the water to propel us forward.

"I can't paddle when you're doing that." I groaned as she pushed down against me. "I can barely fucking think."

"Have I finally found your weakness?" She grinned, but her eyes were glazed over in pleasure.

"You've always been my weakness, Frankie." I paddled harder, and I had no fucking clue what direction I was taking us in. I just knew that I needed to get out of this damn boat and somewhere where I could touch her properly.

The canoe hit the bank, and Frankie looked behind her. "This isn't the rental place."

"I don't care." I stood with her in my arms and almost knocked us both out of the boat.

Frankie squealed and tightened her arms around my shoulders and her legs around my waist. I looked past her to try to get an idea of where we were, but all I could see were trees. The sun was barely providing any light at this point, but it didn't matter.

I wasn't sure if anything would have stopped me. Anything but her.

I climbed out of the boat, my foot sinking into the lake as the canoe tipped almost fully over, and Frankie laughed.

"We didn't think this through."

"I told you I couldn't think at all." I lifted her higher against me to get a better hold, and she looked around.

She reached between us and pulled her shirt over her head. She tossed it into the boat before looking back at me. "Then let's not think."

I walked farther into the water, and I didn't give a shit that I was fully dressed. Frankie kissed me as the warm water hit her calves, and I sank down into the water as her tongue slid over mine.

She was wearing the thinnest black bra I had ever seen, and I rolled my hand over her breast just as the water reached it.

"You are so goddamned perfect." I looked up at her before lowering my head and running my tongue over the soft curve of her breast.

"You have a biased opinion."

"I don't." I shook my head and pressed my mouth against the fabric of her bra. Her nipple pebbled in my mouth, and I ran my tongue over it gently before jerking the cup down and exposing her.

She let out a shocked moan, and I sucked her nipple into my mouth.

"Olly." Her fingers tangled back into my hair as I grazed my teeth against her. "I'm so wet."

I groaned against her chest and dropped my hands from her waist to find the button of her shorts. I slid my hand beneath the rough fabric, and she whimpered as my fingers grazed her clit.

"God, I love your pussy." I worked my way back up her chest and neck, and I captured her mouth with mine before murmuring my next words against her lips. "I love how I lose all control just by touching you."

I ran my middle finger over her clit, and she cried out against my mouth.

"You're like the sweetest fucking sin, Frankie." I wrapped my arm around her back and forced her harder against me as I continued working her clit. "I'm not sure how I'm ever supposed to give you up."

I slid my hand lower and sank my finger inside her as I pressed my palm against my clit. She rolled her hips and rode my hand.

"Olly, I don't want to come like this." She rode my hand even harder, and I knew that she was close. "I want you inside me."

"Not tonight, Frankie. We don't need to do this. Not here."

"Yes." She pushed off me, and I was forced to pull my hand from her shorts as she stepped back. "Here."

She walked out of the water, and I watched as she pulled her soaking wet shorts and panties down her legs. She turned toward me before reaching around her back to unclasped her bra.

"I don't want to wait anymore."

I followed her out of the water and struggled as I pulled my wet t-shirt over my head. I would be lying if I said I didn't want to be her first. Of course, I did.

But I didn't want to take any more from her.

I wanted her to have more than this.

"Frankie." I ran my hand over my face as I tried to think clearly.

"Fuck me, Olly. Please."

I threw my t-shirt down on the ground behind her before reaching out for her and lifting her against me. I dropped down to my knees on the bank and lowered her in front of me.

I ran my hand down her stomach, and she trembled beneath my touch.

Her knees were bent in front of me, and I spread them apart until her knees were touching the ground. I pressed a kiss to the inside of her thigh, and she moaned.

Her back arched off the ground as I kissed my way toward her pussy, and I looked up to see her staring straight at me.

I didn't look away as I kissed the top of her slit or as I ran my tongue through her. I spread her pussy apart with my fingers and sucked her clit into my mouth as she dropped back to the ground.

"You taste so fucking good." I slid my fingers into her as I ran my tongue over her clit. "I could eat you for every meal, and I still wouldn't have enough."

Her legs shook at my sides, and she attempted to close them against me.

"Keep your fucking legs open, baby."

"I'm going to come." She pressed them harder against me, and I curved my finger inside her. "Oh, God."

"Legs open or I stop." I let my words rumble against her.

Her legs fell back to where I put them, and she leaned up to look at me. She bit down on her bottom lip as I grazed my teeth over her clit. "I want to come with you."

"You will." I pumped my fingers in and out of her. "But first you're going to come against my face."

I fluttered my tongue against her clit, and her legs shot back up and pushed against my shoulders as her pussy clamped down against my fingers. She was so fucking beautiful as she came, and I didn't stop moving my mouth against her until I watched the pleasure course through every inch of her.

I lifted back onto my knees and settled between her thighs. She ran her hand over her mouth before pushing up onto her elbows. I leaned forward and kissed her, and she wrapped her hand around the back of my head. She held me against her as her mouth moved frantically against mine.

"We don't have to do this," I whispered against her mouth. "There's no rush."

"I want to." She reached down and pushed my shorts down my hips until my cock sprung free. I was so fucking hard, and I pressed against her wet pussy with a deep moan. "I want you to be my first."

I pulled back from her and slid my cock up and down her pussy. She was so fucking ready for me, her pussy dripping after the way she had just come, and I watched my every move against her.

"I want to be your first too, but we don't have to do anything you're not ready for. I don't want you to think you have to do anything more than just be yourself to make me happy."

Everything about her felt so perfect. She felt like so much more than anything I had ever felt before, and I tried not to think about why that was.

"Olly, stop." She tightened her hands against me and forced me to look up at her. "Please don't make me feel wrong for wanting you."

I kissed her then with my heart hammering in my chest, and even though I still felt unsure about what we were doing, about her not regretting me, I felt desperate for her.

"Frankie, I..."

"Erase him, Olly." She didn't look away from me as she said it. "I want you to completely erase everything he ever did to me. This is my choice, and I want it to be you."

My chest swelled with pride not only because she was choosing me, but because I knew how much courage this took. Her bravery was the most goddamned beautiful thing about her.

"I choose you."

I ran my hand down her chest as I leaned back and stared down at her. This was her choice, and I had to stop trying to think I knew better than she did when it came to protecting her.

She was more than capable.

And for the first time, I realized that while we were all too busy trying to shelter her, she was busy becoming stronger and stronger.

There wasn't an ounce of uncertainty in her eyes, and I wanted to taste every bit of her fearlessness. I craved to be burned by it until she messed me up so completely that I wouldn't ever be able to walk away.

And that was fucking reckless.

I kissed her hard before I pulled my wallet out of my pocket, and laughed when I pulled out the wet leather along with my phone.

"Well, that's fucked." I tossed it on the ground and pulled the condom out of my wallet.

"Oh well." Frankie chuckled and ran her hand slowly up and down my cock.

"Fuck." I held on to her knees as I felt weak on my own. Her hand was so damn soft, and she used it to run my cock back up and down her pussy. She tensed as I hit her clit, and I could see the desperation in her eyes.

I ripped the condom open with my teeth and slid it over my cock. I hated that there was going to be anything to separate us. For the first time in my life, the thought of not using a condom flashed in my mind, but I would never do that to her.

I was already being selfish enough.

I pressed the head of my cock against the center of her, and I hesitated there as I ran my thumb over her clit. She jumped against me, but I didn't stop. I knew this was going to hurt her, but I wanted her to enjoy it as much as she possibly could.

"Tell me if it's too much." I pushed into her gently, just an inch. "You tell me, and I'll stop."

"I know you will, Olly. I trust you."

My hips shot forward the smallest amount at her words, but I restrained myself. I didn't know how she could trust anyone after the things that were taken from her, but it hit me in my gut that she trusted me.

I slid into her slowly, inch by inch, and I focused on her clit with every movement. She pushed her hips against me, trying to force me further, faster, but I pressed my left hand against her hips to hold her in place.

She was breathing heavy, and I leaned forward and drank in every breath as I fully pushed inside her.

"Are you okay?"

"Yeah." She nodded rapidly, and her chest shook beneath me. Regardless of what she said, she was nervous, and I wanted to do everything I could to take that away.

I kissed her slowly and thoroughly as I started to move inside her, and she dug her fingers into my back.

"You feel so good." I murmured my words against her neck and tried to catch my breath. Sex had never felt like this with anyone, but being with Frankie made me feel like I was drowning.

I held on to her, clung to her, as I tried to clear my head, but one simple thought kept flashing through my head.

I love her.

Fuck, I knew I did. I had known it for what felt like forever, but this was different. It swelled inside of me in a way that made my chest ache with longing.

Even after I left, once this was over, I knew that Frankie would leave a mark on me that would haunt me. She would be the girl I always looked for, the one I would never be able to find again.

But I couldn't tell her any of that.

"Olly, please." She tightened her legs around me and wrapped her hand around her breast. "I need more. Please. Please don't act like you're going to break me."

This was her first time, and even though I knew I wouldn't break her, I wanted to do everything in my power to make sure I didn't hurt her.

But she pressed her heels into my back and used them as

leverage to move her hips against me. She felt so damn good, too good, and every bit of logical thought slipped through my fingertips with every move she made.

I leaned back and watched where we connected, and my hands shook as I placed them on her hips. "Lift your hips for me, baby."

She did as I asked before placing her fingers against mine and digging them into my skin. She was looking up at me in the same way that I knew I was staring down at her, like we were both drowning in all the things we couldn't say, and it was enough to push me over the edge. I was so damn close to coming, but I refused to until I watched her fall apart around me.

I slammed into her, before slowly pulling back out, and the soft whimper that left her mouth drove me crazy. I repeated the move over and over as her pussy clamped down around me, and my fingers dug in her hips as I grasped for control.

"Olly." My name sounded like a prayer, and I picked up speed and used my left hand to pull her thigh higher against my side. She was so open for me, so wet, and I ran my other hand down her pussy until I felt where we met.

"Oh God," she whimpered and slammed her head back against the ground as she closed her eyes. I slowly raised my hand and brought my thumb back down against her clit, and as soon as I put the smallest bit of pressure there, she arched her back off the ground and her thighs tried to close around me.

I held on to her, my hand on her thigh and my other rubbing small circles, and I leaned down and pressed a soft kiss to her knee. Her eyes flew back open to meet mine, and she looked so wild with lust in that moment.

It was the most beautiful I had ever seen her look. There were no pretenses between us, no hiding what we felt, and even though I knew I should've been careful, I allowed myself to soak in every bit of emotion she was giving me.

Because even through the lust, I knew that this was more.

Sex had never been like this. It shouldn't have been like this between us, because I knew it was going to make it impossible for us to quit each other.

But I didn't see a way to stop it.

"Fuck, Frankie. I…" My stomach tightened and I pressed my fingers into her thigh as she clenched around me. "I…"

"Oh my God."

I couldn't think past the way her mouth opened and her eyes slammed shut. I watched her orgasm course through her like I could trace every inch of its movement, and it dragged my own pleasure from my body so quickly, that I wasn't prepared for it.

I slammed inside of her over and over as I came, and her thighs trembled at my sides. My heart was racing to the same erratic beat of her body, and I ran my fingers over her neck as I tried to calm myself down.

It was overwhelming. Everything about her and the feeling that was clawing at my chest, and I knew I was in such dangerous territory. I wanted more from Frankie. More than I was able to take. More than we had agreed to.

She leaned forward and caught my lips with hers in a lazy kiss. I was still seated inside of her, and everything suddenly felt like more than it was just a moment ago.

This was sex, Olly. A summer fling. That was what Frankie called it, and that was what I needed to remember.

She was my best friend's little sister, and fuck, she had become one of my best friends.

And I was going to screw this all up. Even without Beck, even if he didn't kill me for what we were doing, I knew I wouldn't survive her.

I didn't know how I was going to survive walking away.

CHAPTER 9
FRANKIE

I plopped down on the couch and laid my head against my mom's lap. She smiled down at me before running her fingers through my hair.

"You seem happy." She slid her finger slowly down my nose, and I relaxed against her. The soft scent of her warm perfume which she had worn all my life hit me, and I took a deep breath.

"Okay." I laughed softly. "I am happy."

"Did something happen? Or have you met someone?" she asked hesitantly. My mother and I rarely talked about boys, and I knew that it was because she thought it would trigger me. She didn't want to talk to me about boys because I could still see the hurt in her eyes when she did. "You just seem happier than normal."

I turned in her lap until my face was facing her belly and shrugged my shoulders. I didn't want to lie to her, but there was no way I could tell her the truth about Olly. Not only would she tell me it was a bad idea, but she would worry about me. And I was so tired of them worrying about me.

"No." I shook my head gently against her. "I'm just happy. It's summer. I've been able to spend so much time with my friends, and I don't know." I shrugged again.

She continued to run her fingers through my hair, and it was something she had always done. I didn't know how such a simple touch from her could put me at so much ease, but it did. I always had.

"It's okay." She laughed quietly. "You don't have to explain your happiness." She watched me with so much adoration in her eyes. "I just like seeing you this way. That's all."

"What are we talking about?" Beck leaned over the back of the couch and stared down at the two of us.

"Nothing," I answered quickly, and my mom laughed.

"You were definitely talking about something." Beck narrowed his eyes at me, but I simply stuck out my tongue at him.

I couldn't quite explain it, but I felt like Beck could tell there was something different about me. It had only been a couple days since I had gone out on the lake with Olly and given myself to him, but I felt like I didn't even recognize the girl I was before then.

And it wasn't just the sex.

It was something else, something that felt like it had snapped into place when Olly was touching me, and I didn't know what it was.

Or maybe I did. Maybe I knew that the moment I chose Olly and allowed him to touch my body in a way no one else ever had that it healed something inside of me. Something that I tried to pretend wasn't broken.

I trusted Olly, and watching him touch me and honoring

that trust, shoved down every bit of fear I had been trying to hide.

It was like taking a deep breath after slowly suffocating for years.

But this was supposed to be fun, and I was happy. I didn't want to think about what was going to happen in just a few short weeks.

I didn't want to ruin the way I felt right now with worrying about the reality of what we were. Because I knew that it would ruin it. It would destroy everything.

But I wasn't ready to let go. Not yet.

Not after what we shared the other night or the way he held me after or kissed me like he was feeling as wrapped up in the feeling of us as I was.

"Firstborns are always busy bodies." My mom reached up and patted Beck's face.

Beck frowned, and I couldn't help but smile. "First of all, that's rude. Second of all, you're a firstborn too, Mom."

"I'm well aware." She nodded and looked back and forth between us. "That's how I know."

"Uh-huh." Beck rolled his eyes before knocking his hand against my knee. "Do you want to go with me?"

"Where are you going?"

"Some of the guys are getting together for a flag football game. Josie's meeting me there from work."

It was on the tip of my tongue to ask him if Olly would be there too, but I knew he would question me. He would question why I cared.

"Yeah." I nodded and sat up on the couch. "Can I change clothes first?" I was wearing a pair of black shorts and an old t-shirt, and even though Olly had seen me like this a hundred times, I wanted him to think more of me than he had before.

"No." Beck looked down at me like I was crazy. "It's flag football, not prom. I'm already going to be late. Let's go." He leaned down and kissed my mom on the forehead, and I grabbed my tennis shoes off the floor and slid them onto my feet.

"Bye, Mom!" I called out to her as we made our way to the door.

"Be careful!" She yelled back the same thing she always told us as we left the house. "I love you both."

We both said our I love yous before Beck shut the door behind us. We climbed into his car, and I quickly fastened my seat belt.

The two of us were quiet as Beck drove, and I almost jumped out of my skin when he finally talked. "What's up with you?"

"What are you talking about?" I looked over at my brother before quickly looking back at the road.

"I don't know. You're acting weirder than normal."

"Maybe it's you who is acting weird." I crossed my arms over my chest.

"Uh-huh." He eyed me curiously, and the smallest bit of sweat coated my palms. "I'm sorry if I've been spending too much time with Josie."

"What? No. I love Josie."

"I know you do, but you're still my sister. You and I spent a lot of time together before her." He ran his fingers through his hair as he glanced over at me, and I could tell that he had been thinking about this a lot. And I absolutely loved him for it.

Because even though his overbearing ways drove me

crazy, I knew that everything Beck did was because he loved me and worried about me.

"Trust me, I am so much happier now that I have Josie. And Allie. I feel like I finally have friends."

"Hey." He knocked his hand into my shoulder. "I've always been your friend."

"That's different. You're my brother, so you have to be my friend." I rolled my eyes at him just as we pulled up to the park.

"No. I don't." He turned off the ignition. "I genuinely like hanging out with you, whether you're my sister or not. So do Olly and Carson. They both love you."

His words struck me in my chest even though I knew he didn't mean them the way my heart was taking them. They loved me like Beck loved me. They loved me as their friend.

"I've been actually hanging out with Olly a lot lately." I pressed my fingernails into my palm as I spoke. I didn't know why I said it, but part of me wanted to know what he thought about me and Olly. What he would do.

"I know." He nodded and grabbed a gym bag out of his back seat. "Don't tell Carson this, but Olly's the best." He laughed softly. "I'm glad you have him as a bonus brother. I'm glad you have them both."

A deep ache hit me in the pit of my stomach as he talked. Olly wasn't my brother. He wasn't even close, but I still nodded my head. Of course, I was glad that I had him too, but I just wished that I could be honest about everything.

"Come on." Beck opened his door and climbed out. "Everyone's waiting on us."

I climbed out of the car behind him and ran my fingers through my hair. There were several guys on the old field, half of them in shirts, half of them not, but I couldn't see Olly.

We made our way down to the field, and I took a quick seat beside Josie and Allie on the ground. Josie tossed me a Gatorade and a bag of chips as soon as my ass hit the ground, and I laughed.

"Always prepared."

"If we're going to have a show" —she waved her hand out toward the boys— "we might as well have a snack."

Beck leaned down and pressed his lips to hers. "I better be the only show you're watching."

"Oh, yes." She nodded dramatically. "Of course, I'll only be looking at you when Olly's standing back there looking like a Greek god without his shirt on."

I knew she was joking, but I searched him out and, fuck. She was right. He was laughing at something someone was saying, but I barely even noticed his face. He was standing there in a pair of black gym shorts that hung low on his hips, a pair of white tennis shoes, and nothing else.

I knew that anyone who looked at me would know exactly what I was thinking as I stared at him, but I didn't stand a chance in hiding my reaction to him.

He ran his hand down his chest absently as he talked, and God, I had never wanted to be a hand so badly in all my life.

I slowly traced my gaze up his body until I reached his face, and I jolted back when I saw him grinning at me.

Shit. He just caught me ogling him.

He made his way over to us, and I quickly looked away and unscrewed the cap on my Gatorade. I needed to do something to distract myself. If we still didn't want anyone else to know about us, then tackling him on this field and getting my hands on every inch of him wasn't a good idea.

"Finally." He stood next to Beck, and I stared straight ahead at his shoes. Don't look up. Don't look up. "We're ready to start, but the other team is one player short. We'll have to take it easy on them."

"They couldn't find anyone else to play?" Beck asked as he pulled his shirt over his head and tossed it down beside Josie.

"No. They said they tried everyone."

"I'll play." I opened my mouth before I really thought it through.

"What?" Beck and Olly both answered at the same time.

"You're not playing." This one came from Olly.

"Why not?" I pushed off the ground and wiped the grass from my shorts. "Don't be sexist idiots. I know how to play football."

"We're skins, Frankie." Olly smiled at me like that was a simple solution. "And you sure as shit can't take your shirt off to play with us."

I lifted my shirt and showed them my hot pink sports bra, and Olly jumped in front of me as if I was flashing the world. "Technically, I could, but I wasn't offering to be on your team."

"You're going to play against us?" He chuckled and stared down at me. His chest was so close to mine, and my hands trembled against my shirt with the urge to touch him.

"Well, if I'm going to play, I'd like to be on the winning team."

He grinned so hard that it made my breath catch in my chest, and he narrowed his eyes at me. "Okay, smartass." He nodded. "Let's see what you've got."

I followed them onto the field and smiled as Olly introduced me to the other team as their new teammate and watched them collectively groan.

Guys were such assholes.

"Okay." One of the guys finally talked to me once Olly and Beck were on their side of the field. "What position do you think you can play?"

"Receiver." I shrugged my shoulders. "I'm fast. Just throw me the ball."

I saw one of the guys roll his eyes, but I didn't care. They could think whatever they wanted about me.

We started the game, and sure enough, not a damn person threw a ball within twenty yards of me.

I was so frustrated that I was about to tell them I quit, but then the other team snapped the ball, and I watched as my brother tossed the ball in Olly's direction. I was on the opposite side of the field from him, but none of these guys stood a chance in catching him, and he knew it.

He ran down the field with a smirk on his face, and I took off in his direction. He didn't even glance my way, too busy watching the guys that were still attempting to come for him, and he stumbled hard to the side as I ran into him.

His gaze hit mine just as he hit the ground and I landed across his chest.

"Oh my God," he groaned, and I heard laughter ring out around us.

My knee was barking with pain from the way it hit the ground, but I ignored it. I was too busy staring down at the naked chest that was plastered underneath my hands.

"Frankie, are you out of your mind? You could have been hurt." He was still groaning, and I leaned up on my elbow to look down at him.

"You could have been hurt." I laughed. "You're the one lying on the ground groaning."

"This is touch football." He widened his legs, and my body slid beneath them. I could feel his cock just beneath my stomach, and I knew he could feel me too. His hips surged forward the tiniest bit before he sat up and pulled me up with him.

I kneeled between his legs, and I couldn't help looking down at his shorts. "Are you okay?"

"Who are you asking?" His question was so quiet I barely heard it. "Me or my dick."

"Both." I grinned at him. "You're both so important to me."

"Shit, Frankie. Are you okay?" Beck reached out for me, and I took his hand and let him pull me to my feet.

"I'm fine." I laughed and looked around. "Can't a girl tackle the guy with the ball when the rest of you couldn't catch him?"

Olly laughed as he climbed to his feet and rubbed his side.

"Did I hurt you?" I lifted his arm and inspected the side of his torso, but other than a few grass stains, he looked fine.

"Just my ego." He chuckled, and I looked up at him with a smile.

"You all need your ego knocked down from time to time."

"Uh-huh." He grinned and pointed to the quarterback on my team. I couldn't remember his damn name even though he had already told me twice. "Give her the ball next time. Let's see what she can do."

He listened too.

The next play I took off down the field like I had been doing the entire game, but this time, he actually threw the ball in my direction. It sailed over my head, and for a second there, I didn't think I was going to catch it.

But the ball landed in my hands and I tucked it into my side with a smile before I took off running harder.

It was my mistake that I didn't look around. I was still on a high from catching the damn ball, and I didn't see Olly until I ran square into him. He didn't stop there, though. He tucked his shoulder down and pressed it into my hips.

The wind was knocked out of me as he lifted me into the air and continued running. I screamed as I clung to the ball and wrapped my other arm around his torso. I couldn't see anything other than his ass as he ran, and honestly, I wasn't complaining.

He ran all the way to the opposite end of the field before he dropped me to my feet, and I pushed my hair out of my face as he tried to catch his breath.

"That wasn't fair." I looked back down the field at everyone coming in our direction.

Olly held up his arms near his head and yelled, "Touchdown!"

"That was not a touchdown." I narrowed my eyes and pressed my hand into my hip.

"Yes. It was." He grinned but he was still breathing hard. "I intercepted the ball and ran it all the way down the field."

"No." I shook my head. "You intercepted me."

"Either way." He shrugged his shoulder and laughed. "But this way I got to touch you while I show you how strong I am."

"Oh my God." I clutched my stomach as I laughed. "I really did hurt your ego."

"No." He stepped closer to me and tucked some stray hair out of my face before he whispered, "You made me hard as a rock while I'm playing football with a bunch of my friends, and I was dying to fucking touch you. They are all staring at you, and I'm ready to beat the hell out of all of them."

My gaze snapped over to him just as he ran his hand down the front of his shorts because it was as if he had forgotten where we were and who we were with. "I can't wait for this fucking game to end."

That was all I could think about as we finished the game, what he had just said, the way he was looking at me.

And he never seemed to look away after that.

He dropped two balls that were thrown his way, and I couldn't help but laugh as I walked by him and patted him on the shoulder.

It was probably a mistake because the moment the game was over, Olly was still looking at me like he was ready to eat me alive.

"Better luck next time." Carson knocked his shoulder into mine, and I rolled my eyes.

"Yeah. Yeah." I rolled my eyes. "You all are such humble winners."

"We try." Beck laughed and nodded to his car. "You ready?"

"Yeah." I nodded and glanced over at Olly.

"I'm actually going to take Frankie to get a bite to eat." He pulled his t-shirt over his head, and I frowned. "We made a little wager before the game, and she lost, so my dinner is on her."

We did no such thing, but I didn't argue. I would have agreed to anything to get alone with him.

"We're going somewhere cheap." I pointed my finger at him and grabbed my drink from the ground.

"All right." Beck smiled and there wasn't a bit of suspicion in his eyes. "I'll see you back at the house."

Olly and I sat there until almost everyone else was gone, and we barely said a word to one another. He just kept bumping his knee into mine, and I bit down on my lip as I stared over at him.

"Let's go." He stood and reached down for me. I let him pull me to my feet, and I was surprised when he didn't drop his hand from mine as we walked to his car.

He opened the door for me, and I finally pulled my hand from his as I slid inside.

I bounced my leg as I watched him walk to the driver's side.

"Where are we going exactly?" I asked as soon as he closed his door.

"I hadn't really thought that through." He chuckled and leaned his head against his headrest as he turned to look at me. "I just wasn't ready for you to go home."

I wasn't thinking as I leaned forward and pressed my mouth to his. I just knew that I couldn't take another second without kissing him.

His hands tangled in my hair, and he pulled me tighter against him.

"I've fucking missed you." He breathed against my mouth.

"I've been with you for hours."

"It's not the same." He shook his head, and I knew that he was right. He kissed me again, his lips and tongue tasting me in a way that I knew he was trying to commit the feeling to memory. Our time together was almost up, and we would miss this.

I was going to miss everything about him.

He pulled away from me slightly, but he still held me in his hands as he stared down at me.

"Let's go get you some food."

"Okay." I nodded my head, but I couldn't look away from his mouth.

"Frankie, you have to stop looking at me like that if you want me to be able to drive."

"Right." I glanced away, then looked right back.

"You are trouble." He leaned forward and kissed me again, and I honestly didn't care if I never ate again as long as he kept kissing me. The more his mouth moved against mine, the more I felt like I was starting to care less about anything that wasn't him.

And that was dangerous.

I pulled away from his kiss and settled back into my seat as I tried to clear my head.

"All right, all-star. Feed me."

CHAPTER 10
OLLY

I was being foolish. The last few weeks with Frankie had made me almost forget everything outside of her, but I was leaving in a week and reality was here to slap some sense into me.

I stared over at Frankie, and she smiled at me. Her entire face was lit up, and I knew that what was going to happen next was going to break her. It was going to break both of us.

But we didn't have any other choice.

We promised each other that this thing happening between us was temporary. It was for the summer. But every part of that felt like a lie.

It was just how we convinced each other that what we were doing was okay, that our lies weren't that bad.

Now we were sitting together on the beach with my heart hammering in my chest, and I couldn't figure out how to string a few words together.

"What's wrong?" She ran her fingers through the sand, smoothing it out before raking her fingers back through it. "You look pissed."

"I'm not pissed." I shook my head. I didn't know what I was.

Fucking confused.

"You could have fooled me." She reached up and ran her finger between my brows. "You look so grumpy."

I tried my hardest not to smile, but the way she was studying my face made it pointless. "I'm not pissed. We just need to talk."

"Oh." Her smile fell along with my chest.

"You know I'm leaving next week," I said the words so softly that I wasn't sure if she heard them. It was like if I didn't say them loud enough, then they wouldn't actually come true.

"I know."

"And—"

"And what?" she cut me off. "I'm not an idiot, Olly. I know what that means."

"What does it mean?" I wished she would tell me because I didn't have a fucking clue what that meant.

She shook her head without answering, and I knew that she was as frustrated with our reality as I was. Because neither one of us wanted this to end.

It didn't matter what we promised or the expectations we set at the beginning. None of that mattered now. Not anymore.

But I couldn't bring myself to believe that because everything about her mattered. It always had.

"You're leaving, Olly." She shrugged her shoulders like it was that simple.

"But..." I hesitated because I didn't know what to say. I didn't know how to explain to her exactly what I was feeling, but I could have sworn that I saw it staring back at me. And that was what killed me the most, because we could never be.

Not like this.

Not some giant secret that we'd hidden from everyone. Frankie deserved far better than that, and we both knew it.

"We both know that we can't keep this up." I reached out for her, and she watched the way I touched her with a hesitancy that I hated.

"I know." She nodded, but there was so much pain in her eyes when she looked up at me. "You're going to be gone, and I can't expect you to not want to be with other girls."

My chest tightened at her words. This was the last thing I wanted her to feel. "It isn't like that."

"It is." She nodded her head and pulled away from my touch. "And I understand. You're going to college, and I'm still in high school. You can't be expected to not live your life because of this little fling we had this summer."

I knew that she was protecting herself, but her words sliced through me regardless.

"And you should have fun during your senior year." I pressed my hand into her side and tugged her toward me. Her body was stiff at first before she melted under my touch. "You have prom and so many guys who are dying for a chance with you." My hand tightened against her, and I knew she felt it.

"You're right." She nodded. "I should be with other guys. Date, fool around."

My hand tightened even further, and I felt like I was losing control. "Frankie."

"What?" she pushed, and I could see the spark of fire in her eyes. I was hurting her, and she refused to let me see it. Frankie was so tired of being hurt that the only thing she knew now was to fight. "That's what we agreed to. This one summer, then you can fuck whoever you want to and so can I."

I slammed my mouth down against hers because I refused to think about her being with anyone else. She was mine.

Fuck.

She would always be mine regardless of what decisions we made.

Frankie pushed her fingers into my hair and straddled my lap as she tugged on the strands. She was angry, and I was okay with that. I could handle her anger or whatever else she needed to take out on me.

Because I was angry too.

I wrapped an arm around her back and forced her as close to me as I could get her. My other hand wrapped into her hair, and I tightened my fingers into the strands just at the base of her skull. She moaned against my mouth as I ran my tongue across her lips.

She moved her hips against mine as she kissed me, and I felt like I was going to go insane from the movement.

"Frankie, we're on the beach." My words were muffled against her lips, but they didn't slow her down at all.

She just moved harder and faster against me, and her hands tightened as if to hold me in place.

"I need you."

Something snapped inside of me at her words, and I couldn't stop what was happening between us if I wanted to. I was too far gone, and I needed her as badly as she needed me.

I feared that I would always need her.

I slid my hand beneath her tank top and cupped her

breast in my hand. She sucked in a hard breath as her chest rose and fell at the same speed as her hips. I rolled her nipple between my thumb and finger over her thin bra as I bit down on her bottom lip, and she cried out against my mouth.

"You are so goddamned beautiful." I kissed her again, harder than before, and she kissed me back with just as much need.

It was still pretty light outside, the sun slowly falling, but I didn't care. Nothing was going to stop me at that moment. Nothing had ever really been enough to stop me from her.

Even though it should have been.

We had plenty of reasons for this not to happen, but I couldn't think of a single one when she was kissing me.

I gripped her ass in my hand, and I forced her harder against me as she moved. She moaned, and I knew she could feel how hard I was beneath her.

Her stomach trembled as my hand slowly slid down her skin. Every inch felt softer than the one before, every second making my breath catch harder in my chest. It hit me that this could be the last time I ever touched her like this.

This could be the last time she felt for me what she was feeling now.

Because regardless of what I did or didn't want to hear, the reality was that Frankie was going to find someone else. Maybe not immediately. Maybe not in this fucking town with a school full of people who didn't deserve her, but eventually she would.

She would find someone else, and I would have no choice but to let her go for good. Because even now, even saying what we'd said, I knew I wasn't letting her go. Not really.

And I wasn't sure if I could.

I dropped my hand until I cupped her pussy over her shorts, and she whimpered against my mouth. She was so damn responsive. I pressed harder, my fingers digging into the fabric, and I moved my palm against her clit.

"Are you going to miss me when I'm gone?" I asked, and her gaze snapped to mine.

"You know I am."

"I'm going to miss you too." I kissed along her jaw, and she dropped her head back to give me better access. "And I'm going to miss this." My tongue rolled over her neck, and I could feel her rapid heartbeat beneath my touch. "I'm going to miss the way you moan my name."

She tensed above me before she began moving harder against my hands, and I knew that my words were turning her on as much as my hand. They always had.

"I'm going to fucking crave the taste of your pussy." I nipped her earlobe between my teeth. "And the way you come against my face."

"Olly." She turned her head and tried to bring my mouth back to hers, but I was sinking lower, my mouth pressing against the soft curve where her neck met her shoulder.

"I've never tasted anything sweeter in all my life." I sucked her skin into my mouth to prove my point. "And I doubt I ever will again. Your pussy was made for me, Frankie."

"Oh my God."

I could feel how wet she was through her shorts, and I wasted no time tugging them to the side and burying my fingers inside her. They slid through the moisture so easily, and I curved them forward inside her over and over as I chased her orgasm that belonged to me.

"I'm going to come." She warned me as if I didn't already know. I knew her body better than I knew almost anything else, and she would come when I wanted her to, when I changed the speed of my fingers to match that of her hips. My thumb began a pattern of small circles against her clit, and I watched the desperation in her face before she fell over the edge so quickly.

She buried her face in my neck to drown out the sound of her cries, and I didn't stop my movements. I wanted more from her. I wanted all she had to give, and I refused to walk away from her until I had every ounce of her that I could manage.

Because she was mine.

I moved her to her knees beside me, her legs shaking as I helped her into the sand, and I moved behind her. Her back pressed against my chest, and I knew she could feel my heart racing against her.

I looked up to make sure there was no one around us, no one that could see what was mine, but there wasn't a soul. It was just me and her and this thing between us that neither one of us fully understood but lied about constantly.

Because that's what we had become. Nothing but a fucking lie.

I lied to her when I told her that I could do this only for the summer.

I lied when I said that I could give her up.

And the biggest lie of all was when I convinced myself that I wouldn't be completely destroyed when I walked away from her.

I pressed a gentle kiss to the back of her neck before wrapping my fingers around the front of it, and I lifted her until her back fully pressed against my chest and my knees were cradled inside hers.

"I need to be inside you."

"Yes," she whimpered as she pushed her ass against me, and it was enough to ruin me. "Please, Olly."

I jerked my shorts down my hips before doing the same with hers, and I fucking loved the way her bare skin felt against mine. It was like every part of her was made for me. Made with the sole intent to drive me fucking crazy.

I pushed my cock against the curve of her ass, and she tensed before another small whimper left her mouth. I pressed another kiss to the back of her neck. This one lingering. "I want this too." I moved my cock up and down the seam of her ass before stopping just at her entrance. She was so wet that I moved against her easily, and the urge to claim this part of her body along with the rest was overwhelming. "I want to own every fucking part of you."

She nodded against me, not saying a word, but I felt her deep swallow against my hand.

I lowered my cock until I was pushing against her soaking wet pussy. "Do you want that too?" I slowly pushed inside her. "To know that no matter who else ever has you, that you were mine first. All of you?"

"God, yes," she cried out, and I slammed inside her with a lack of restraint that I hated. But that was what she did to me.

Her knees shifted in the sand, and I wrapped my hand around her waist to hold her against me. Her belly trembled beneath my fingers as I lowered them to her clit, and she reached back over her head until her hands grasped the back of my neck.

She was so open like this, so fucking willing to give me

any part of her that I wanted, and I felt like such a selfish bastard at that moment. Because I wanted it all. I wanted to take from her until she had nothing left to give to anyone else, but I knew I couldn't. Because I couldn't give her that in return.

Not like this.

Not like we had been doing things.

And the thought of her getting hurt because I was too big of a coward to be honest with her brother had to be enough for me to let her go.

Because I knew I wasn't strong enough to lose them both. Frankie and Beck were my family, far more than my actual blood, and the thought of losing them made fear slice through me.

"I'm going to miss this." She turned her head until her mouth met mine, and she kissed me with the same desperation that I felt.

Everything about this moment could be our last. The last time I touched her, kissed her, fucked her.

I wasn't ready.

Neither of us were.

"Me too." I slammed into her harder as I kissed her and her pussy clenched around me.

We didn't speak for a long time after that. I wasn't sure if both of us were scared to or scared of what the other would say, but we just relished in each other's bodies.

I tasted every inch of her skin I could reach as I fucked her, and she roamed her hands over my neck and head before moving to my thighs. She was trying to store every bit of me to memory just like I was with her.

I lifted her and turned her to face me as I felt that delicious lick of pain form in my lower stomach. I was going to come, and I needed to look at her as I was doing it. To kiss her, to watch her come around me.

She wrapped her legs around my back as I pressed her into the sand, and I slowed my movements inside her as I pushed her hair out of her face.

I love you.

Those words were so fucking overwhelming at that moment, but I knew they wouldn't be fair to say. But I wasn't sure I needed to. She was searching my eyes like she already knew.

She had to know how I felt about her without me saying a single word, and my chest tightened as I saw that same look staring back at me.

I wrapped my fingers in her hair and ran my nose along hers before I kissed her. And I didn't stop kissing her until her legs tightened around me and her pussy spasmed around my cock.

She gasped for air, our kiss finally breaking as she fell apart, and I had no choice but to chase her over the edge.

I came inside her, the fact that I wasn't wearing a condom not hitting me until that moment, but I couldn't bring myself to care.

I continued to kiss her until her body went completely soft beneath me and I knew everyone would start missing her if I didn't get her home. Even then, I hesitated.

Because no matter how tightly we held on to it, we couldn't keep this lie between us once reality set in.

CHAPTER 11
FRANKIE

I walked into the party with Josie by my side, and I tried to keep my hands from shaking.

This was supposed to be a celebration. A going-away party for not only Carson and Olly, but for half of the other graduating class that was getting as far away from this town as they could.

But none of them mattered.

All I could think about was Olly and how we had spent the last several weeks sneaking around and laughing and falling.

I had spent the entire damn summer falling.

"You look so hot tonight." Josie squeezed my hand as she smiled down at me.

"Thanks." I grinned and attempted to let her words calm my nerves. I had taken extra time getting ready tonight. Extra time to make sure that no matter what happened, Olly couldn't take his eyes off me. Because he was leaving.

He was leaving, and I didn't want him to forget me.

I knew how pathetic that sounded.

He was leaving, starting his new life in California, and I just wanted him to stay. Even though I knew that wasn't what was best for him.

He had been dreaming of leaving this place, and still, my stomach shook with so much anxiety over him leaving that I could hardly take a deep breath.

"Well, look who's here."

My gaze snapped up to meet Lucas's at the sound of his voice. He was looking back and forth between me and Josie, and I tightened my hand in hers as my ability to breathe became even harder.

I hadn't seen him since school ended in the spring, and I didn't expect to see him here tonight.

"What the fuck do you want, Lucas?" Josie's spine was stick-straight, and I knew she hated talking to him almost as much as I did. The difference was that Lucas rarely had the balls to speak to me anymore. He knew the consequences he would face if he did, but he looked like he had been drinking enough already tonight to not care about anything.

"I didn't realize I couldn't say hi to my dear old sister." He grinned at her before his glazed-over eyes met mine. "And beautiful Frankie, of course."

"Don't talk to her." Josie tugged me closer into her side. "Are you out of your mind?"

"I'm leaving, Josie." He leaned back against the wall, his crossed feet blocking our path. "There's not much your little boyfriend can do when I'm no longer in this town."

"Where are you going?" Josie sounded genuinely curious, and I knew that she still had to be so hurt by her father and everything he had done. She rarely ever talked about it, talked about either of them, but I knew that it still took its toll.

"College." He chuckled. "You'd be going too if you stayed at home instead of playing Beck's little whore."

"That's enough." I gripped Josie's hand in mine and started forward. I didn't care what Lucas had to say. I wasn't going to stand here and listen.

I went to step over his feet, and he raised one leg higher to block me. I opened my mouth to tell him to move, but he was staring at me so intently that it made my chest ache. This guy used to be my friend, he was my brother's friend, he was someone I was so damn infatuated with once upon a time that it physically hurt, and he destroyed all that. He had destroyed me.

But even though anxiety rocketed through me as he stared at me, I found that I wasn't nearly as affected by him as I once was. Lucas used to hold so much power over me, and it appeared that some of that power had been lost.

"If you're looking for Olly, he's out back." He nodded his head toward the back of the house. "But I wouldn't be in a rush, the last time I saw him he looked pretty fucking lost in some blonde."

His words slammed into me like a weapon, and I knew he knew they hit his mark by the smirk on his face.

"I'm not looking for him." I shook my head.

"From what I've heard, that's all you're about these days. Does your brother know you're interested in another one of his friends? You just trying to fuck your way through them?"

I froze as the words passed his lips, and it didn't matter that Josie was still holding my hand or that I could feel her anger seething off her. She was one of my best friends, and I hadn't even told her the truth.

But Lucas had just spit it at me like he knew everything.

"You don't know what the fuck you're talking about." Josie moved forward and shoved his legs out of the way until he was forced to straighten.

He didn't care. He just smirked at me with the knowledge that I had just let him get to me, and he was savoring the taste of that on his tongue.

This boy who had done so much to me already was still taking pleasure in any pain he could cause me.

He motioned his hand to let us pass, and Josie tugged me behind her as she hurried past him.

"He's such a douchebag." She stopped once we were far enough away that I could no longer see him. "Are you okay?" Her hands ran over my face. "I'm sorry he said that to you. I'm sorry he talked to you at all." She was looking me over as if she was looking for physical evidence of the pain he had caused.

"I'm fine." It was the truth and a lie. I didn't care what Lucas thought of me anymore. That realization hit me hard. I had cared, but this summer with Olly had taken that away without me even knowing.

But what he knew about me and Olly did. He knew things that I had been keeping from my brother and my friend.

"Let's go find the boys."

Josie started to walk away, but I stopped her with my hand on her arm.

"Wait. I need to tell you something."

"Okay."

"What he said about me and Olly..." I hesitated, and I hated that I felt the need to. She was one of my best friends.

"It doesn't matter what he said."

"It does." I shook my head and tried to make sense of the thoughts that were bombarding me. "He's right."

"Frankie, you don't have to explain anything." She stepped closer to me so no one could overhear us. "I know about you and Olly."

"What?" My gaze snapped up to meet hers. "How?"

"How could I not?"

"Does Beck know?" My heart rate spiked as I thought about how my brother would react. About how he would see this as nothing but a betrayal.

"No." She shook her head, and I could see the guilt in her eyes. "I don't think so, at least."

"He'll hate me after everything that happened with Lucas." My voice shook with the fear of what Beck would think, and I knew that she could hear it.

"No, he won't." She reached up and tucked a piece of my hair behind my ear. "He'll be hurt that you all have hidden it from him, but he'll forgive you."

I took a steadying breath as I let her words sink in. "I'm sorry to put you in this position."

She smiled at me, and I knew that she felt pity for me. "I'm sorry that you felt the need to."

I nodded my head because I wished the same. But I was too far into it now to wish for anything different. I knew what I was doing when I started this, and there was nothing I could do now to change it.

We pushed through the crowd together to get to the back porch, and I spotted Olly as soon as we made our way out. He was leaning against the deck railing with a beer in his hand and a smile on his face, and even though I wanted to be angry with him for leaving, for leaving me, I couldn't.

"There they are." Beck stood and pulled Josie to him. She

laughed as he buried his face in her neck, and I tried to avoid hearing whatever he was whispering in her ear.

I could barely hear a thing over the roar of my heartbeat.

Olly smiled up at me as I walked in his direction, and I attempted to smile back before moving to the other side of Carson and Allie. He hadn't done anything wrong, but I couldn't just stand there next to him and pretend like everything was okay.

I couldn't pretend like I wasn't in love with the guy who was leaving.

And that Lucas didn't know.

"What's up, Frankie?" Carson bumped his shoulder into mine, and I smiled up at him. I could tell by the way he was looking at me that it wasn't convincing.

"Nothing much." I shrugged and pulled out my phone to distract myself. I wish I hadn't come. This was their last hoorah, then they would be gone in a few days, and we should be having the most epic night ever.

But I couldn't.

My hands shook against my phone, and I could barely make out what was on the screen.

Allie reached out and squeezed my hand in hers, but I didn't look up. I knew if I did, I wouldn't be able to control my emotions. I was flooded with fear. Fear of Olly leaving, of all of this blowing up in our faces.

I continued to stare down at my phone as I heard them all talking around me, and I took a steadying breath. I could do this. I only needed to fake this for a few more days then everything would be fine.

Olly: Are you okay?

I stared down at the text without looking up at him. Was I okay? Of course, I wasn't okay. I wanted to scream my answer for everyone to hear, but instead, I quickly text him back.

Me: I'm fine. Just tired.

I tucked my phone into my back pocket and looked over at Beck as he was telling a story about something stupid they had done when they were younger. It was a story I had heard a million times before, and I just wanted to leave.

"Well, if it isn't my old friends."

My gaze snapped to Lucas where he now stood in front of us with his arms open wide. He had the biggest grin on his face as he stumbled forward a step, and it made me so damn nervous.

Lucas had always made me nervous, but this was different.

Beck stood quickly, moving in front of me along with Olly.

"What the fuck are you doing here?" You could clearly hear the venom in my brother's voice, but Lucas just smiled. If I hadn't seen pictures of what Beck had done to Lucas after everything happened, I would dare say that Lucas wasn't scared of Beck, but I knew differently.

"I'm here celebrating graduation just like the rest of you." He looked down the line at all of his old friends before his gaze stopped on my brother. "I thought I might give you a proper goodbye since you're staying behind."

Beck's back straightened, and I knew he was letting Lucas's words get to him. He acted as if Beck was staying in Clermont Bay because he was some sort of deadbeat when the reality was the exact opposite. Beck stepped up for our family in a way that Lucas couldn't imagine.

"Go the fuck on." Olly's voice shook, and I knew that he was angry that Lucas even dared speak to us, to me. He pressed his back against my front, trying to block me from Lucas's view, and I tightened my hands in the back of his shirt.

"You have some fucking balls on you, Warner." Lucas chuckled, and Olly went stiff under my touch.

"What the hell is that supposed to mean?"

"Just let it go." I tugged on Olly's shirt harder to get his attention, but his eyes were solely on Lucas.

"It means that you all act like you're better than everyone else." Lucas cocked his head to the side and stared at Olly. "But you've got secrets of your own. Don't you?"

When Lucas's eyes shifted to me, I could feel the fury coming off Olly. I should have warned him about what Lucas said. I should have known that Lucas would do anything in his power to hurt me.

"As do you." Lucas winked at me, and I could feel the shift in the air.

Olly jerked out of my touch, and he was in Lucas's face before anyone could stop him. He fisted Lucas's shirt in his hand and slammed him back against the house. Lucas didn't drop the smile from his face for a second even as the back of his head slammed into the hard exterior.

"Don't fucking speak to her." Olly's voice was shockingly calm as he spoke to Lucas, but I knew him well enough to hear the fury beneath.

"Oh right." Lucas laughed and looked back in my direction. "I wasn't allowed to touch her, but you are, right?"

"Do you have a fucking death wish?" Beck stepped forward, and I felt like everything was collapsing around me. I didn't know how to stop this. I didn't know how to breathe.

"Beck." I reached for his hand, and his angry gaze met mine. "Please just forget about him and let's go home."

I didn't want to do this. I didn't want Lucas to bring up the memories of the worst night of my life or how idiotic I had been, but more than anything, I didn't want him to fuck everything up even further.

"How does that work, Beck?" Lucas called out, and no matter how tightly I was pulling Beck toward me, he still looked back to him. "You suddenly okay with your best friends fucking your sister?"

"What the fuck are you talking about?" Beck growled, and I could feel tears welling in my eyes. *No, no, no, no. This couldn't be happening.*

"Your sister and your boy here." Lucas looked at Olly. "Right under your nose all this time. She's sweet, isn't she, Olly?"

I could barely keep up with what happened next as Beck jerked his hand out of my touch, and I watched Olly rear back before slamming his fist into Lucas's face. There was a loud commotion all around us as the people at the party were all raring for a fight.

Lucas slammed his elbow into the side of Olly's face before tackling him to the ground. The deck shook as the two of them slammed against it, but I jerked backward before I could really see what was happening. Carson shot past me and hit one of Lucas's friends that was trying to get to Olly.

Allie wrapped her arm around my shoulders and I jumped. She tugged me against her as panic ensued. I looked up at Beck, but he was frozen in place, his gaze never wavering from where the fight was happening.

"Beck," I called out his name, but he didn't look in my direction.

My voice seemed to stir something inside him, though,

and he finally moved. He shot forward into the fray of people, and I watched as he grabbed Lucas by his collar and jerked him off Olly.

"Shit." Josie moved beside us and ran her hands over my face. "We should get out of here."

"I'm not leaving." I shook my head, and my eyes met Olly's. He pushed himself up off the ground just as Beck kneed Lucas in the stomach, causing him to double over in pain.

Olly said something to Beck, but I couldn't hear a word of it. Beck shoved Lucas out of his way, and he took a step toward Olly. I still couldn't hear them, but it was easy to spot how furious Beck was. And this time, the fury was pointed directly at his best friend.

I pulled away from Allie and Josie and made my way toward them. Josie called out for me, but I ignored her as I moved forward through the chaos.

I was almost knocked on my ass as someone was shoved into me, but I kept going.

"What the fuck do you want me to say?" I finally heard Olly's words as I made my way closer to them.

"I'm going to kill you."

I pushed in front of Olly just as Beck spoke those words and pressed my back into his chest. "Beck, stop."

"Are you sleeping with him?" He was staring at me like he barely even recognized me, and I knew that Olly and I had fucked up by keeping this from him.

We had more than fucked up.

"It's not like that."

"Then what is it like, Frankie?" Beck laughed without an ounce of humor, and he was speaking so loudly that I knew everyone could hear. "He fucking promised to protect you, and now he's fucking you behind my back."

"Beck..."

"I would do anything for her." Olly's sharp words surprised me.

"Except take care of her without putting your dick inside her." Beck was no longer looking at me.

"I'm right here, you know, and I don't need a fucking babysitter."

Beck's gaze snapped to mine, and I knew he wanted to tear into me, but I'd had enough. Yes, we kept something from him that we shouldn't have, but that didn't give them the right to treat me like they did.

"You all act like I'm some fragile doll who can't live her fucking life." I pushed off Olly and stepped forward. "Are you all going to alert me when I am finally allowed to date or fuck someone, or am I going to be the girl who got assaulted for the rest of my life?"

Beck jerked back at my words, but I wouldn't take them back. I had meant what I said. The way they treated me did nothing but give me a reminder of what happened every single day.

"We don't treat you like that."

"Yes. You do." I clenched my hands into fists. I was so frustrated that I wanted to scream. "There is nothing wrong with me wanting to be with Olly."

Any bit of anger I had taken away before came back full force, and I knew that Beck wasn't going to let this go.

"Is that what Olly told you he wanted?" He waited for an answer, and when I didn't reply, he kept going. "He's fucking leaving, Frankie. How is he going to be whatever the fuck he's convinced you of when he's not here?"

"Beck."

Beck pointed his finger at Olly. "Don't you dare fucking speak to me. You are no better than him." He looked over to where Lucas still leaned against the house clutching his already bruising jaw. He was smiling despite his pain, and I knew this was exactly what he wanted.

"I can't believe you just said that," I barely whispered the words, but neither one of them were listening to me anymore.

"What do you want me to say?" Olly held out his hands. "I'm not Lucas. I care about her. Frankie is more than capable of making her own decisions. I would never do anything to hurt her, and you know it."

"That's why you took advantage of her." Beck shook his head. "You knew that she trusted you, and you took advantage of that trust. You were meant to protect her, and instead, you became the exact thing you were meant to protect her from. Don't ever touch her again," Beck growled and I tensed. How dare he?

How fucking dare he think that he got to make those kinds of demands?

"You've already been dealt one shitty family. You touch her again, and you lose your second one."

I could see the fear in Olly's eyes. Beck knew it too. He hit Olly exactly where he knew it would hurt him. He hit him in a place that would force him not to choose me.

"Okay." Olly's voice was weak as he said it.

"What?" I stepped away from him, but Olly wasn't looking at me. He was staring straight ahead at my brother. "How dare either of you." I looked back and forth between them.

"Frankie, this is between us." Beck wasn't looking at me either.

"No. It's not," I practically screamed, and I silently begged Olly to stand up for me, for us. "This has everything to do with me."

"Frankie, you..." Beck sighed, and my heart raced.

"I'm in love with him."

I felt Olly stiffen, but I didn't look in his direction.

"I'm in love with him, and it doesn't matter whether or not you think that's okay. It's not going to change the truth."

Beck looked back and forth between us, and I could feel everyone else watching us too.

"And what about you?" He jerked his chin in Olly's direction.

"I..." Olly hesitated, and I finally let my gaze meet his. He looked so confused, so damn conflicted about what he was supposed to do, and my heart broke a little at that moment.

"I'm nothing." I finished his sentence for him. "Olly and I had agreed before we even started this. This was nothing more than this summer and then he was going away to college." I smiled up at him and prayed he couldn't see how badly I was hurting. "I'm the idiot who took things too far."

"Frankie." Olly reached out for me, but I pulled my hand away from his touch.

"I'm going to head home." I took a step back and ran straight into Carson. I patted him on the chest with hands that shook and tried to avoid the way he was looking at me with so much pity. "Will you take me?"

"Of course." He nodded and slid my hand in his steady one.

I looked back at Olly, and I wished I hadn't. He was looking at me now like I had wanted him to a moment ago.

He was saying things with that one simple look that he had been too cowardice to say out loud.

But it wasn't enough.

I tightened my hand in Carson's as I turned back in his direction, and I walked away.

CHAPTER 12
OLLY

It had been two days since the party, and I felt like I was going crazy.

Because it had also been two days since I saw or heard from Frankie, and even though I text her, there wasn't a single reply. Not that I could blame her.

I had been a complete and total asshole at the party, but I didn't know what to say or do. I didn't know how to explain to her brother that I was in love with her even though I had promised him that I would always do everything in my power to protect her.

I had failed him.

I had fucking failed them both.

I knew that was the truth before, but it hit me like a ton of bricks when I heard her tell him that she loved me. She loved me, and I was too big of a coward to say it back.

Because I knew that Beck's anger was real, and when he threatened that I would lose my family, my real family, I froze.

Because that was what I had really feared all along.

"Fuck." I ran my hands through my hair as I stared up at their house. I had been sitting in my car for the last ten minutes, and I still hadn't gathered up enough courage to get out.

I watched as Beck stepped out of the front door and looked over at me with a blank look on his face. He still hadn't forgiven me for what happened, and I couldn't blame him. I knew what I had been doing, and I knew the consequences I would face.

But in my stupidity, I thought we could get away with it.

I climbed out of my car just as Carson stepped out of the house behind Beck. I was thankful he was here even if he didn't deserve to be in the middle of this.

"Hey," I called out before sitting against the hood of my car.

"What are you doing here?" Beck asked, and his voice sounded so dead.

"I came to talk to you. To talk to her." I nodded my head to where I knew Frankie's room was.

"You're not talking to her."

"Beck, you are my best friend, but she's been one of my best friends for a long time too." I crossed my arms over my chest. "I need to talk to her."

"And what are you going to say?"

"That I'm fucking sorry." I was honest with him for the first time in a while. "I'm going to tell her that there aren't enough words to tell her how sorry I am."

Beck shook his head, and I knew that he wanted to lay into me. He had done plenty of that after Frankie had left the party without letting me get a single word in, but he wasn't done.

"You hurt her."

"I know I did."

"And you're an asshole." He stepped closer to me.

"I'm aware of that too."

"To be fair." Carson took a seat beside me. "Both of you are assholes, and both of you hurt her."

Beck stared at me, and I didn't look away. I would take whatever it was he felt like he needed to do or say.

"I'm sorry that we didn't tell you."

He didn't say anything for a long moment. "But you're not sorry that you did it."

"Do you want me to be honest with you?"

"For once."

I let his dig slide over me and nodded my head. "Then no, I'm not sorry that it happened, and I can't act like I am."

Beck nodded his head slowly, and I knew that probably wasn't the answer he was wanting.

"I care about Frankie a lot, and I've been interested in her for a long time."

"How long exactly?" He cocked his head to the side and looked at me.

"Before Lucas."

Beck stared at me, and I had no idea what he was thinking.

"But you're leaving tomorrow." He didn't say it with any venom in his voice. He was just stating the truth, and I hated that it sliced through me like the worst insult.

"I know."

"And this is her senior year in high school. She can't keep up a relationship with you while you're across the damn country and she's trying to figure out who the hell she is. She's finally living after what happened with Lucas." He shook his head.

"I know that too."

"So what was your plan?" He crossed his arms over his chest and stared down at me.

"Honestly, we just wanted to have fun together." I held up my hand when I saw the anger creasing his face. "It wasn't just about sex. We enjoy being around each other."

"You're really not helping your case," Carson muttered and knocked into my shoulder.

"Do you really think I would have risked you being this angry with me if I didn't fucking care about her?" I held out my hands and stood. "You can be mad if that's what you need to do, but you cannot stand here and act like you don't know that I love your sister. She has been one of my best friends for years."

"And now it's going to break her that you're leaving."

"She knew I was leaving." I tried to convince him and myself that it made everything okay. "We both are more than aware of that fact. Trust me, the last thing I want to do is hurt her."

Beck took a deep breath, and I looked back up at the house. Was she in there? My body buzzed with adrenaline as I thought about marching up to her room and demanding that she talk to me.

I needed to see her, to talk to her. I was desperate to.

"If you don't want to hurt her, then you have to stop this. You can't let her think that this is going to go any further than this when it's not."

"Okay," I said the word, but it tasted like acid in my mouth. It wasn't okay. I couldn't pretend like I didn't want anything from her after today. Like I could just forget that the last couple of months hadn't happened. I wanted to be with her, truly be with her, but I didn't think it was something that would ever really happen.

"And you can never do this again."

I looked up at him, and the urge to tell him to fuck off was on the tip of my tongue. Beck was one of my best friends, but I couldn't imagine never touching or feeling or loving Frankie again.

"That's a little harsh," Carson said from behind me, but Beck wasn't listening to him.

"If you want our friendship to work, then you promise me. Frankie's been through enough already, and you fucking with her head is the last thing she needs."

I could barely catch my breath as I thought about what he was saying, but maybe he was right. Maybe I was doing nothing but hurting Frankie, and I couldn't keep doing that to her.

"Okay." I nodded my head as I tried to convince myself. "I promise."

Carson let out a deep, frustrated sigh as the front door opened, and all three of us turned just as Frankie stepped outside. She shielded her eyes from the sun as she looked at me, and she was silent for a few tense moments.

"Can I talk to Olly, please? Alone."

I wasn't even sure what Beck or Carson said as they answered her. My attention was solely on her, and I couldn't look away.

When the two of them stepped inside, Frankie finally stepped off the porch and moved toward me. She looked so damn beautiful even though her eyes held a sadness that gutted me, and the urge to reach out and pull her toward me was overwhelming.

"I text you."

"Yeah." She tucked her hands in the back pockets of her jeans and looked over at my car. She stopped so far away from me, and I hated it. "I know. I've been busy."

We both knew that was a lie, but it was one I let her get away with.

"Okay, well." I ran my fingers through my hair as I racked my brain for any of the million things I had thought about saying to her. "I'm sorry about the other night."

She looked back at me, and she looked so void of emotion. She looked so unlike the Frankie I knew.

"It's not a big deal." She shrugged. "He was bound to find out sooner or later, and it's probably for the best that it happened now."

"I'm not so sure if I agree with you about that." I shook my head, and she laughed.

"You should. It just makes everything easier."

"How so?" Why did my heart feel like it was about to burst through my chest?

"We don't have to make each other any false promises once you leave and make this entire thing awkward. We both know exactly where we stand." Her mask slipped as she said those words, and I saw the sadness hiding beneath.

"And where is that?"

"Don't act stupid, Olly. It doesn't suit you."

I could feel panic setting in along with my anger. "Well, you clearly have this figured out, so why don't you tell me."

"I'm just going off what you said." She looked up at her house, then back at me. "Or were you just promising my brother that we'd never do this again and hoping I didn't hear you?"

"Frankie." My hand shook as I tried to reach out for her.

"No." She shook her head and pulled away from my touch. "You don't get to do that anymore."

"We both agreed that this was for the summer." I tried to rationalize what the fuck I was saying and the stupid decisions I was making that were causing my chest to ache.

"I'm well aware. You didn't promise me anything."

I opened my mouth to speak, but she wasn't finished.

"But you have been my best friend for a long time, and I expected... hell, I don't know what I expected. More." She looked up at me, and her eyes were burning with all the emotion she was hiding earlier, and it slammed into me with an intensity I wasn't prepared for.

"And I wish I could give you that."

"It doesn't matter."

"It does."

"Let's not make this worse than it needs to be." She motioned back and forth between the two of us. "We are friends, and we will always be friends first. I don't want a few months of lust to ruin that."

I hated that was what she had boiled us down to because we were so much more than that. We were so much more, and I couldn't do a single thing about it.

So, she was right.

I wouldn't lose her, not as my friend, and I had to man the fuck up and deal with the consequences of my actions.

"So, what? We just go back to normal and pretend like none of this ever happened?"

"Exactly." She shrugged again. "I don't really see any other choice."

I wanted to tell her that I couldn't imagine going back to being what we were before now that I had tasted every damn inch of her perfect body, but I knew that wasn't fair. She was offering me the easy way out, and I needed to take it.

"Plus, you're going to be across the damn country." She held her arms wide as if to indicate how far apart we'll be. "I will be the furthest thing from your mind."

"I honestly doubt that." I stepped even closer to her because I couldn't stand how far apart we were. I wanted to grip her face in my hands and force her to look up at me until I could see every bit of emotion she was trying to hide from me. My chest ached as badly as my hands.

"Are you still going to come to visit me?"

"If you still want me to." She looked so unsure as she said it, and I hated that I had given her that hesitation. I had made her doubt herself.

"Of course I do."

"Okay." She nodded and tucked her hands back in her pockets. "I definitely have to come watch a game because I'm sure you'll be starting."

"I'm a freshman, Frankie."

"It doesn't matter." She shook her head and a small smile formed on her lips. "You're incredible."

She was splaying me open with her words, and I wished that she was yelling at me instead. I wanted her to tell me that I hurt her and that I didn't fucking deserve to breathe the same air as her because that was the truth.

But instead, she still believed in me. She believed in me more than anyone else ever had. More than my parents and even Beck and Carson. She had become my safe place far more than I had ever been hers.

She had become the one person who I could be completely real with, and now all of that was going to change.

"I really am sorry," I whispered and grabbed her hand in mine before she could pull it away. "I wish things could have gone differently. I wish we could be... fuck... just different."

"Me too." She nodded and stared down at her hand in mine. "But we can't."

She leaned up on her tiptoes and held the side of my face as she pressed a gentle kiss to the other. "Give them hell in California."

"I'm not leaving until tomorrow." I turned to face her, and our lips were so damn close. It would have taken nothing for me to lean forward the slightest bit and close the gap between us.

"I know, but I'm not..." She hesitated and stared at my mouth. "I'm not sure if I can handle seeing you again before then."

I took in a shuddering breath and ran my gaze over every inch of her face. I wanted to remember her like this, when she still felt for me what I was feeling for her.

"I..." I reached up and cupped her face, and the urge to tell her the truth was so overwhelming. "Frankie, I..."

"Please don't say it." She shook her head and took a step back. "I'm really proud of you."

"Frankie."

Three more steps. "Please text me and let me know when you make it to Cali." She made it all the way to the door before she turned back in my direction. "Goodbye, Olly."

CHAPTER 13
FRANKIE

I hated this stupid school.

That was all I could think as I pushed through the crowd of students in the hallway who didn't know how to get out of the freaking way. I needed to get to my locker to get my English book, and I was going to scream if the girl in front of me didn't stop giggling and get a move on.

We were three weeks into my senior year, and everyone kept telling me that this was going to be the best year of my life. But it didn't feel like it.

All of my friends had graduated, and I didn't have anything in common with these people. I didn't want to.

I just wanted to go home and hang out with Josie and Allie and try not to think about Olly. But that was all I could seem to do. Even the two of them couldn't distract me from thoughts of him for long.

Everything seemed to always take me back to him.

"Excuse me." I shouldered past the girl and finally made it to the front of my locker. I spun the lock until I entered my combination and jerked my locker open.

"Hey, Frankie."

I looked over at Connor as he leaned back against the locker next to mine. I had gone to school with him for years, but I didn't really know the guy.

I didn't want to either.

"Hey, Connor. What's up?" I grabbed my English book out of my locker and shoved it into my already full backpack.

"I just wanted to see how you're doing. You have Jones for AP English as well, right? We're three weeks in, and she's already brutal."

"Yeah." I nodded. I didn't think she was brutal at all. Tough? Sure. But I don't know what else he expected in an AP class at a private school our parents paid an arm and a leg for. "She's keeping me busy. That's for sure."

"That's actually what I was going to ask you." He shifted nervously, and I braced myself for whatever he was going to say next. "I was wondering if you might want to go out this weekend."

"I'm sorry." I shook my head. "I'm busy this weekend."

"With Olly?" he asked as he ran his hand through his light hair. "I thought he moved away for college."

"What?"

Don't think about him. Don't think about him.

Don't fucking think about him.

"I know everyone's been talking about what happened between you and Olly at that party, but I thought he left."

Heat rose up my chest, and I could feel it coating my cheeks. "He did leave."

He left. He left, and my chest hadn't stopped aching since he had.

"Okay, cool." He grinned like my answer was exactly what he was looking for. "I'm open whenever you are."

"I'm not interested." I pulled my backpack up onto my shoulder before closing my locker.

"I thought you said he was gone." Connor looked so confused, and that pissed me off.

"Olly Warner has nothing to do with whether I want to go out with you or not."

He straightened off the locker, and I watched his face morph from what I was assuming he considered charming to angry. Boys like Connor weren't used to being told no.

But I didn't care.

"You don't have to be such a bitch."

I knew he was trying to get under my skin, but he was going to have to do better than that. Because I felt absolutely nothing at his comment.

I felt nothing at all.

"Thanks for asking, Connor." I patted his arm as I passed him by and headed straight for my English class. It was my last class of the day, and I was so ready to get it over with.

I was so ready to get out of this damn school where I could stop pretending like everything was okay.

I pushed into the classroom and took my seat before pulling out my book and my notes. Mrs. Jones was still sitting at her desk looking over some papers, so I quickly pulled out my phone to check it.

I had one text from Josie telling me that she talked my mom into tacos tonight. I sent back a quick hell yes before I opened Instagram and searched for Olly's name.

I chewed on the side of my thumb as I waited for it to load, and I looked around to make sure no one was watching me.

There was one new photo posted today, and it was a simple shot of him and Carson on the field in their practice gear. He had the biggest grin on his face, and it made my chest ache.

I wanted to be with him. I wished that I was the one that was making him smile like that.

But neither one of those things was possible.

The caption below his photo made me smile.

First practice as a Golden Bear.

My finger hovered over the screen before I finally clicked that little red heart. I knew that he had to be excited. He had been looking forward to this day for what felt like forever.

And even though I had barely spoken to him since he left, it didn't mean that I didn't wish for his happiness any less. I just wished things were different.

Part of me wished that I had never crossed that line with him at all, but I knew that I really didn't mean that. But it was easy to convince myself that I did when my chest was aching, and I felt like I couldn't breathe.

It was my first thought when I heard him promise Beck that he would never have this thing with me again because it would have been easier that way. If I could just forget about him for five damn seconds, everything would be easier.

I could have concentrated on my class instead of tapping my pencil against my book and staring ahead at nothing until the bell rang.

He was hundreds of miles away from me and still I felt like I couldn't breathe.

I stuffed everything back into my bag and pushed out of the door as quickly as I could. When I stepped out into the parking lot, I still felt like I couldn't get a deep enough breath.

I climbed into my car and threw my bag in my front seat before rolling my windows down and cranking up the radio.

I tried not to think of anything as I let the music flow through me, but it was impossible. It was as if every lyric was written about him, and it was driving me crazy.

I turned it off completely as I pulled up to the house, and I was relieved when I saw both Josie's and Allie's cars in the driveway. The two of them were the only things that seemed to be able to distract me from my racing thoughts.

Even if it was only for a few moments.

I had to make it enough.

Because without them, I felt like I was drowning. I was drowning with Olly gone, and I didn't know how to change that.

I didn't know how to be okay without him here.

Because everyone else acted like nothing had ever happened. Beck wasn't angry with me at all. All his anger was directed at Olly as if I didn't have any ability to make my own choices, and I hated it. Because I did choose Olly.

Regardless of if that hurt Beck or not.

And I hated that he just went about his day-to-day like nothing had happened. Like his best friends weren't gone, and that I felt like I was dying inside without Olly.

It was all I could think about as I climbed out of my car and planted a smile on my face. I wasn't okay but would pretend until I learned to be.

CHAPTER 14
OLLY

"You're going to have to leave this apartment at some point." Carson leaned over the back of the couch, and I pulled my attention from the TV to look over at my friend.

"What are you talking about? I leave all the time."

"I meant for something other than class or practice." He knocked his arm into my shoulder. "Come on. We're going out."

I looked at him, then back at the game that was on TV. "I don't want to go out." I didn't want to do anything other than just sit here and try not to think about her.

"That's too damn bad." He stood and grabbed his keys off the counter. "We're going."

The TV went black, and I groaned and looked back over at him. "Seriously?"

"Yes, seriously. You need to get out of this damn apartment and quit moping." He crossed his arms, and I knew he wasn't going to let this go.

"Fine." I huffed and grabbed one of my baseball hats off

the table. I pushed it onto my head, settling the bill at the back, and stood. "But I don't have to like it."

"Of course not." Carson rolled his eyes and headed toward the door. "But some of the guys are starting to question whether or not you have a hard-on for me since you don't spend any time with anyone else."

"You're so full of shit." I followed him out of the apartment and into his car.

"Where are we going exactly?" I clicked on my phone and stared down at the screen. There wasn't a single missed message, but I wasn't surprised. Frankie hadn't messaged me in weeks, and when I messaged her, she barely replied.

And even though I knew that was what should be happening, it still made me fucking sick.

"To a bar," he said dramatically. "Don't worry, it's just a couple streets over. You can run home if you need to."

"You're such a dick." I tucked my phone back in my pocket.

"I know." He nodded. "But I hate seeing you like this."

We pulled into a parking lot, and Carson pulled into one of the only spots left.

"I'm fine." I adjusted the hat on my head and climbed out of the car.

Carson followed me out and looked at me over the hood of his car. "You do know that I've been your friend forever, right? You are not fine. You need to—"

"Don't," I cut him off and shook my head. "Whatever you are about to say, just don't."

He shook his head as if he was exhausted by our conversation, and I couldn't blame him. I felt exhausted by it too.

We made our way up to the bar, and it was so damn crowded that people were spilling outside. Music was blaring, and every time the door opened, I was bombarded by the sound.

I didn't want to be here, I didn't want to do this, but Carson was right. I couldn't sit in our apartment and continue to do nothing but think about her.

"Holy shit! You came!" One of the guys from our team clapped his hand against my back and practically knocked me into someone standing next to me.

"Here I am." I looked around the bar, but I didn't really recognize anyone other than the few guys from our team. I knew most of these people probably went to school with us, but I couldn't bring myself to care.

"Someone get this man a drink!" he shouted, and a few cheers rang out around us.

A beer was placed in my hand a few moments later as I grabbed an empty seat at the bar, and I had no idea who bought it. But I did know that I clearly wasn't old enough to get my own, so I quickly downed the cold liquid and tried to calm my nerves.

I tapped my fingers against the bottle and smiled as Carson talked animatedly with our teammates. I pulled my phone back out of my pocket and clicked on Frankie's photo.

The last text from her was a simple *Good luck!*

Good fucking luck.

And nothing since then.

My fingers itched to send her a message now, but I didn't know what to say. I didn't know how to message her and not tell her that I simply couldn't think of anyone else, of anything.

"Oh, excuse me."

I looked up from my phone just as a girl almost knocked

it from my hands. I held out my hand and grabbed her arm to help steady her, and she laughed.

"Oh my God. I'm so sorry."

"You're fine." I set my phone down and smiled at her. She was pretty, and if things had been different, I would have even been attracted to her.

But things weren't different and her brown hair only reminded me of Frankie, and not because it was similar, but because it was so different. Hers was a soft brown that looked so dull in comparison to Frankie's. Frankie's was a shade barely less than black, and even though it was so dark, it shined in a way I couldn't explain.

"This place is too freaking crowded." She pushed some hair out of her face before leaning against the bar beside me. "You can barely walk."

"Yeah." I nodded and looked around. "I don't know how anyone can ever hear themselves think."

"They can't." She laughed and shook her head. "I guess that's part of the allure."

"Yeah. I guess you're right." I lifted my beer and took another long drag.

"I'm Jordan." She held her hand out to me, and I took it. Her skin was soft against mine, and the floral scent of her perfume hit me.

She felt wrong. She smelled wrong.

"Olly."

"It's nice to meet you, Olly." She blinked up at me with a soft smile, and it should have been so easy for me to lose myself in a girl like her. I should have been able to use her to force myself to forget about Frankie.

But I knew that was impossible.

"It's nice to meet you as well. You go to the university?"

"I do." She nodded. "I'm a sophomore. You?"

"Freshman."

"Oh shit." She laughed. "A younger man."

I smiled, and it felt like the first genuine one to cross my lips in what felt like forever. "I can't be that much younger than you."

"Let me guess." She tapped her jaw and tilted her head from right to left as she studied me. "You're a jock. Football, perhaps."

"You're half right."

"Which means I'm still half wrong." She lifted her drink to her lips, and I did the same. I finished the beer before setting the empty bottle back on the bar. "It must be baseball then."

I chuckled, and she snapped her fingers. "I'm right!" She leaned closer to me, and I braced myself. "I have this talent of spotting a jock from a mile away."

"Do you find this talent useful?" I rubbed my jaw and smiled at her.

"Of course, it is." She tapped the side of her head as she grinned. "A smart girl never dates a jock."

"That feels like a broad judgment." I laughed and spun my empty bottle.

"But it's a well-practiced one." She scrunched up her nose when I laughed again. "That came out wrong. I meant that I have a lot of friends who have dated jocks, and it never ends well."

"We can be a lot to handle, but maybe you've just been with the wrong jocks." *What were you doing, Olly?* I looked at her, then back down at my phone.

Jordan was pretty and, admittedly, she was funny, but she wasn't enough to make me forget about Frankie. I could never forget about her, and even as Jordan laughed and responded to what I had just said, guilt flooded me.

I wasn't doing anything wrong, and still, I felt like I was betraying Frankie.

"Can I get another beer?" I asked the bartender as he walked by, and he dropped one on a napkin in front of me before grabbing my empty.

"See, that right there is one of the biggest problems with jocks. You're probably what, eighteen, and still he just hands a beer over like it's nothing?"

"And how did you get your drink?" I nodded to the one still in her hand before taking a calming sip. "Older friends." She winked and laughed. "Speaking of. I should go check on them."

She hesitated and looked back over at me.

I could tell she wanted to say something, and my stomach dropped as I waited. I didn't know what she was going to say, and I also didn't know if I wanted it or not.

She turned toward the bar and grabbed a pen before turning back to me. She grabbed my hand in hers before she glanced up at me, and she bit down on her bottom lip as she wrote her number down on my palm.

"Use it, jock." She grinned, then dropped the pen back to the bar and took a step into the crowd. I lost sight of her before I could even answer her.

I stared down at her number for what felt like forever before I lifted my phone. My hands shook as I stared at her number, but I clicked my phone on before I lost my courage.

My phone was still opened to Frankie's last message, and my chest ached as I stared down at it.

Fuck.

CHAPTER 15
FRANKIE

Olly: I miss you.

Frankie: Yeah.
Frankie: I miss you too.

CHAPTER 16
FRANKIE

"I don't think I should have come." I wrapped my hand around the handle of my bag and tried to calm the way it tremored around it.

"He's going to be so happy you're here. Trust me." Allie smiled at me, but I couldn't help thinking she was wrong.

She had been begging me to come to California with her for weeks to visit Carson and Olly, but I had barely spoken to him. I wasn't sure what came over me and made me say yes, but I knew that I missed him more than I was worried about my own self-preservation.

Or what Beck thought.

Because he wasn't happy.

But he couldn't expect me not to be friends with Olly anymore, and I couldn't continue to make choices based solely on what everyone else wanted.

Even if I was unsure.

Because here I stood on their damn doorstep, and my gut told me that this was a bad idea. What if he didn't want me here?

Allie raised her hand and knocked on the door, and my heart raced in my chest.

"This was a bad idea."

Carson opened the door wearing nothing but a pair of gym shorts and a sleepy look on his face. I didn't blame him. It was already ten o'clock, and I knew that they had practice today.

"Holy shit!" He reached for Allie and tugged her straight into his arms. I watched as he held her against him, and it was impossible to miss the way tension left his body with that one simple touch. "I'm so fucking happy you're finally here."

He opened his eyes and looked at me, and from the way he jerked back as if he had seen a ghost, I was guessing he hadn't noticed me at all when he opened the door and spotted Allie.

"Frankie, is that really you?"

"In the flesh." I shrugged with my bag still in my hand.

Carson let Allie go and pulled me into him, but every bit of the tension that had left him a moment before was back. "I had no idea you were coming to visit."

"Neither did I." I stepped back from him and tucked my hair behind my ear. "Kind of a last-minute decision that Allie talked me into."

He looked over at his girl, but I couldn't see the look that passed between them. "Well, come on in." He grabbed my bag before grabbing Allie's, then motioned for the two of us to go inside.

There was a too-large TV on the wall that was currently showing some superhero movie and a large sectional couch that sat directly across from it. The apartment was decorated sparsely, and I couldn't help but smile as I noticed some of Olly's things lying around.

"Is Olly here?" I asked and watched as Carson looked down the hall and back to me.

"He is." He nodded. "But he…"

It was at that moment that I heard her giggle, and I was still staring at Carson as my breath left me in a rush.

"Cool." I barely managed to squeak out the word. "It's late anyway, and it was a long flight."

"Frankie."

"Do you care if I use the bathroom, then maybe use the couch for the night?" My hands were starting to shake and I felt like everything in that tiny apartment was closing in on me.

"Of course not." Carson pointed down the hallway to the door that sat in the middle. "The bathroom is right there."

I took a step toward it before Allie grabbed my hand in hers. "I'll come with you."

"No. I'm fine." I shook my head and prayed that the tears that were welling in my eyes weren't visible. "Go catch up with your boyfriend."

I pulled my hand from hers and headed to the bathroom before she could object, and I locked the door as soon as I entered.

The smell of him hit me almost instantly. I wasn't sure if it was his body wash or his cologne or the mix of the two, but it made my chest feel like it was splitting open.

He was in there, in his room, with another girl. I didn't know what I had expected to walk into, but that reality had been so far from my thoughts that I hadn't even considered it.

And I was an idiot.

It had been two months since Olly left for college, and that was two months that he hadn't been with me. Two months that I had felt like I was dying without him, and he was here...

Don't go there, Frankie.

I pushed off the door and moved to the sink. I stared in the mirror as I turned on the water. I looked as sad as I felt, and I hated that it was so on show for them all to see.

I was the sad girl pining over him, and he had already forgotten about me. I was such a damn fool. I don't know what I expected to happen, but deep down I knew that I was still holding out hope that the stupid promise he made my brother didn't matter.

I had hoped that there would eventually be a future for the two of us.

But I was wrong.

I splashed the cold water on my face then grabbed a towel off the rack to dry it. I turned off the water before leaning against the counter, and I could hear rushed whispering outside the door.

I knew they were talking about me, and I could feel heat radiating from my fingers and rushing through every inch of me.

I couldn't stay in here forever regardless of how badly I wanted to. I was going to have to go out there and face them, and I was going to have to do it while trying to pretend like I didn't care about Olly anymore.

Not like I used to.

I took a deep breath and pushed off the counter. I planted a smile on my face as I opened the door, and I hate that it faltered the moment I saw Olly standing near the back of the couch.

He and Carson looked like they were arguing, and they stopped the moment I walked back into the living room.

"Hey, Olly." I grinned harder and forced myself to move toward him. I held my arms out before pulling him into a hug to prove just how okay I was, but it was a mistake. A huge fucking mistake.

His arms wrapped around me, and he held me against him like he was desperate to do so. He held me against him like he had been thinking about me every second of every day like I did him, and my heart couldn't handle it.

His skin was so warm against mine as he held me tighter and pressed his head into the crook of my shoulder, and it felt so familiar in a way that I knew I would never get that same feeling with anyone else.

"Frankie," he whispered my name, and it sounded like a plea. It was almost enough to make me forget everything and beg him for anything, but it couldn't be. Not when his bedroom door opened and a girl stepped out while straightening the bottom of her shirt.

I tensed in Olly's hold before letting him go and taking a step back. He didn't want to let go of me, but he didn't have a choice. I didn't give him one.

"I'm going to head out," the girl said softly while looking at Olly, and I studied her.

She was beautiful. Her hair was the lightest shade of brown, and she was a good five inches taller than me and curvier in a way that made her look like a woman. She pushed her hair out of her face as she walked toward us, and I knew this had to be awkward for her.

I wondered what Olly said. Did he tell her that she had to leave?

"Please don't leave on our account." I touched my chest,

and I could feel my heart pounding beneath. "I'm about to get some sleep anyway."

"It's okay." She looked to Olly, and I recognized that look in her eye. She liked him. A lot, and I instantly felt sorry for her.

Olly didn't give her any indication that it was okay for her to stay. Instead, he was staring directly at me.

"I've got a lot of schoolwork I need to get caught up on." She smiled at me, and I hated that I hated her without even knowing her. But I did. I hated her instantly, and I knew that wasn't fair.

She walked toward the door and stopped when she was directly in front of Olly. I looked away from both of them because I couldn't bear to watch it. I looked over at Allie, and she was looking at me with so much pity that I couldn't take it.

I moved to the couch as I heard the girl whisper something to Olly, then heard him reply. I couldn't make out what they were saying, and I was thankful. I wasn't sure if he hugged her goodbye or kissed her softly on her lips like he used to do with me, and I tucked my hands under my thighs as the image played out in my head.

The door closed with a soft click, and it was dead silent in the apartment. All four of us didn't say a word, and I hated how awkward this felt when we were all supposed to be best friends.

"Do you have an extra pillow?" I looked back at Carson and avoided looking at Olly. "I would love a blanket if you barbarians have one of those as well."

I hadn't been thinking when I didn't pack my own. I guess in my head I had assumed that I would be sleeping in Olly's bed even if I hadn't really let myself go there.

"Yeah." He ran his hand over his hair, and he looked so stressed. I really shouldn't have come. "Let me grab you one."

He moved to his room, and I looked back at Allie and begged her not to leave me alone with Olly. She took a seat beside me without me saying a word, and I had never been so thankful to have her in my life.

Her thigh pressed against mine, and she leaned back into the cushion as she looked over at Olly who still stood by the door. "How has practice been going? Carson said this past week has been brutal."

"It has been." He cleared his throat, but I still didn't look in his direction. I was suddenly completely fascinated by the movie on their TV. "Coach has been kicking our ass with pre-season workouts."

I wanted to ask him if that was why he hadn't had the time to text me lately, but I knew I really didn't want the answer to that. I wasn't being fair, not to either of us, but even as I knew my emotions were irrational, I couldn't stop myself from feeling them.

"Here you go." Carson came back around the corner and tossed a pillow and blanket down beside me.

"Thank you." I pulled the pillow into my lap and pressed it against my chest. It did nothing to calm the ache that still resided there, but I pressed harder and harder and willed it to do something.

"I'm going to head to bed." Allie placed her hand on my thigh. "Do you want me to sleep out here with you?"

"Of course not." I laughed and smiled at her in a way that I hoped she found believable. "Go enjoy your boyfriend." I nodded toward Carson. "I know you miss him."

"Okay." She nodded gently, but I could tell she was hesitant to leave me.

I wanted to beg her to take Olly with her. I just needed to be alone and to remember how to breathe before I could face him, but I knew he wasn't going to let that happen.

Allie pressed a kiss to my forehead as she stood, then her gaze slid to Olly.

"Good night, Olly."

"Night." He sounded closer to me, and I closed my eyes and tried to brace myself for him.

He didn't say a word until Allie and Carson were both in his room and his door closing rang out in the entire apartment.

"Frankie." It was just my name, but it sounded so different on his lips.

It wasn't right.

"Hey." I turned to face him and attempted to smile up at him. "Sorry to burst in on you like this. We really should have told you all that we were coming. I don't know what we were thinking."

"No, Frankie." He ran his hand down his chest. "Fuck, I'm sorry."

"You don't have anything to be sorry about." I stood and grabbed the blanket Carson had given me. I tried not to look at Olly as I shook it out and laid it across the couch.

"Yes. I do." His voice was rough, and even though I hadn't talked to him in months, I could still hear his emotion in it. "You don't have to sleep on the couch."

He took a step closer to the back of the couch, and I tucked my hair behind my ear.

"It's fine. I should have gotten a hotel room."

"You're not staying in a fucking hotel room," he growled,

and anger spiked inside of me at his tone. "You can sleep in my room."

"No." My answer was instant.

"You can sleep in there alone if you want," he reassured me quickly. "I can sleep on the couch."

"No."

His gaze finally met mine, and there was so much that I wanted to say that I couldn't.

"You're not sleeping on the couch, Frankie. Don't be difficult."

"I'm not being difficult," I argued with him and looked toward his room where he had been with her. "But I'm not sleeping in there. Where she..."

I caught myself before I finished my sentence, but the damage was already done.

"Fuck. Frankie, nothing happened."

"Don't treat me like I'm an idiot, Olly." I shook my head and stepped back. "It doesn't matter what happened. You're free to do whatever you want with whoever you want. I don't care. I just don't want to sleep in there."

"It looks like you care." He gripped the back of the couch and his knuckles started turning white.

"And it looks like you don't."

I met his gaze again and his dark eyes bored into me. This wasn't how this was supposed to go. We had agreed that what we had was only for the summer and that things were going to go back to normal between us.

"I'm sorry. I shouldn't have said that."

"Is that what you think?" He moved around the couch, and I took another step back to keep space between us. "Do you really think that I don't fucking care?"

"I have no idea what you think, Olly, but it doesn't matter.

You don't owe me anything." He shook his head, but I didn't stop. "You've kept your promise to Beck, and that's all that matters."

"We both know it isn't."

"I don't know anything." I shook my head and pulled my sleeves over my palms.

"Me and Jordan are just friends. We have a class together."

I winced when I heard her name pass his lips and closed my eyes. "I said it doesn't matter."

"Please just let me explain."

"What is there to explain?" I held out my arms. "You're allowed to be with whoever you want."

"No. I'm not." He shook his head. "Do you really think this is what I want?"

"Obviously, it is, Olly." I didn't know what he expected me to think. "And it's okay."

"I have been going fucking crazy." He stepped closer to me, and I took another step back until I bumped into a wall. "You are the only damn thing I have been able to think about since I've been here. I go to sleep thinking of you, I dream of you, and when I open my eyes in the morning, you're my first thought."

"Don't." I held out my hands to stop him from coming any closer to me, and we both watched as they trembled. "I can't do this."

"Did you really think I came here and just forgot all about you?"

"I don't know what I thought." I was honest with him. "But I know that I've barely talked to you since you left, and even though we both agreed for things to go back to normal, that was the biggest lie either of us ever told."

"You're wrong."

"How so?"

"Me telling you that I would be able to walk away from you at the end of the summer, that was my biggest lie." He stepped forward again until his chest was pressed against my hands.

"But you did."

"I..." He searched my eyes, but I had no idea what he was looking for. "I didn't. Not really."

"Olly." I pressed my hands harder against his chest. "Can we please not do this? You've moved on, and I'm doing perfectly fine. I was just blindsided by seeing her. I just need to get some sleep."

"I have not moved on." He reached out and gripped my elbow in his hand. "And trust me, I have tried. Jordan is..."

"Please just stop. I honestly can't handle you saying her name again." I felt so weak as I admitted that out loud, but I couldn't take it. Every time her name left his lips it was like he was twisting a dagger inside me.

"I won't." He shook his head. "I don't want to talk about her." He slid his left hand against mine and tightly gripped my fingers. "But we have to talk."

"Okay, fine." I nodded my head and tried to pull my hand from his but he refused to loosen his grip. "How is college? Baseball? Is it everything you ever dreamed of?"

"That's not what I want to talk about."

"Too bad." I shrugged.

"Fine." He rubbed his thumb over the back of my hand. "College sucks. Baseball is the only good thing about it. My parents cut me off like they threatened, and I've been working at this little Italian restaurant downtown in the small amount of spare time I have to make money."

I opened my mouth to tell him I was sorry, but he kept going.

"When I'm busy, I can almost pretend like I haven't been obsessing over you ever since the moment I left you, but at night." He shook his head. "I can't escape you. I know that I'm the one who did this. I'm the one who made promises to Beck that I shouldn't have made for you. I just don't know what to do. I don't know how to..."

"Olly," I whispered his name, and the firm grip I had on his chest loosened.

He took advantage of my moment of weakness and pushed forward. His chest pressed against mine, and his hands tangled in my hair. I stared down, but he used his hands to force my head up until I was looking at him.

"I can't..."

His thumb pressed against my lips, and he ran it over them as he watched.

"I fucking need you."

I needed him too, but all I could think about at that moment was her. "That's not fair."

"I know." He leaned forward and pressed a kiss against the corner of my mouth. "But it's the only truth I have."

His tongue ran over my bottom lip, and I whimpered. He didn't stop after that.

His thumb ran over my jaw as his lips came down harshly against mine. I didn't stand a chance of my body not reacting to him, and I opened my mouth and deepened the kiss as I wrapped my arms around his shoulders and pressed my thighs together.

The first taste of him was overwhelming and addictive. Regardless of how much I had thought I missed him, none of it compared to this moment. When I was finally with him again and every part of me remembered exactly what we had lost.

His hand slid down my body before wrapping around my thigh and jerking it up around his hip. He leaned against me, pressing between my legs, and I could feel exactly how badly he missed me too.

He groaned as he rolled his hips and tightened his hand on my thigh.

I didn't hesitate as I lifted my other leg and wrapped it around his waist. He pushed harder against me, anchoring me to the wall, and he devoured my mouth like it might be the last time he got the chance.

And I realized it probably was.

We were doing nothing but stealing another moment that didn't belong to us. Not really.

I wasn't sure if we ever really had a single moment that ever truly belonged to us. We had been nothing but secrets and stolen kisses and hidden touches.

It had never been ours.

I rolled my hips against him, and his hand cupped my ass as he held me to him. I was already so wet, and I was aching for him to touch me.

He bit down on my bottom lip before he leaned back and looked down between us at where our bodies met.

"I'm taking you to my bed."

"I don't want..."

His hand tightened on my ass, and he pressed harder against my center. "There hasn't been anyone else." He ran one of his hands over my jaw before bringing his thumb back to run over my lip. "I haven't done anything with Jordan. Anything."

I winced as he said her name, but relief filled me at the

same time. I knew it was irrational to think he wasn't ever going to sleep with anyone else, but I couldn't handle the thought right now. Not when I was still so in love with him.

He pushed us off the wall and adjusted me better against him. He didn't wait for my answer as he headed to his bedroom and kicked the door shut behind him.

His room was dark and lit only by a small lamp next to his bed. The bed took up most of the room, and when he laid me down on his white comforter that was perfectly made, I looked around and tried to take account of everything I could see.

The space was tidy and didn't have much in it except for a large dresser where a TV was set on top. His baseball gear sat on the floor in the corner, and I spotted the brown leather glove that he had been using for years sitting on top.

Olly lifted my shirt, exposing my stomach, and he pressed a gentle kiss just below my belly button that brought all my attention back to him.

"I'm so fucking sorry, Frankie. I don't know how to tell you how sorry I am." He pressed his forehead against my stomach before looking back up at me.

"Have you kissed her?" I asked the question I was dreading.

"No." His answer was immediate. "I swear we've done nothing. I... I couldn't fucking kiss her."

"Then why was she here?"

"Because she's my friend, and she was helping me with one of my assignments. I've been falling behind." He shook his head. "Everything has just been a lot."

"I don't want you to touch me if you've touched her."

"I haven't touched anyone, Frankie. All I think about is you. I've missed every fucking inch of you." His tongue ran over the spot his lips had just left, and I laced my fingers in his hair. "I'm going to taste every trace of you tonight." He held my eyes as he lowered his head again. "There won't be a single part of you that doesn't remember exactly who you belong to."

His words made my chest ache because I knew they were temporary. I was his, but only for tonight. Only for as long as we could manage to steal. I felt like he didn't see it, that this was the end, but it was. Beck had threatened Olly with his worst fears, and Olly had chosen him over me.

I needed to touch him, to feel him one last time.

His teeth grazed over my hips as his fingers gripped the sides of my yoga pants. I gasped from the slight edge of pain from his mouth, and he jerked my yoga pants and panties down my legs.

He pulled them off, one leg at a time, before lifting my right leg and pressing a kiss to the inside of my knee.

"You are so fucking perfect."

He laid my leg back on the bed, pushing my thigh into the mattress and forcing my legs apart. He stared down at my pussy as he reached behind him and pulled his shirt over his head.

He looked so damn beautiful, tanner than the last time I saw him, and possibly even more defined. I knew that baseball was taking a toll on him, but it was clearly doing things to his body as well.

"You're already so fucking wet for me." His hands ran over my thighs and just before he reached my center, he slowly caressed them back down toward my knee.

"Olly, please."

"What, baby?" he groaned and wrapped his fingers around my thighs.

"I need you."

He flipped me over in front of him in one swift movement until my stomach hit the mattress, and I panted as I looked back at him over my shoulder.

He was lowering his pants as he stared down at my ass, and I gripped the sheets in my hands. My body was thrumming with anticipation of what he was going to do, and I pressed my forehead into the mattress as I tried to calm my racing heart.

"God, Frankie." He groaned behind me, and I jumped when his hands moved around the front of my hips. "Lift, baby." He jerked my hips until I was forced onto my knees, and I felt so open and exposed in front of him.

My legs shook and I adjusted my arms underneath my head.

"Olly, what are you doing?"

"Whatever the fuck I want." His hand cupped my pussy, and I whimpered as he slid a finger through my folds. "And I want you to tell me exactly how it feels, Frankie." He moved faster against me. "There's no one here to stop us. No one to catch us."

I didn't say a word because I was too busy concentrating on his hand, but he wanted an answer.

"Do you understand?" he said, and I could feel his breath on the back of my thigh.

"Yes." I moaned and spread my legs the tiniest bit more as my body begged for his mouth.

"Good girl." He didn't waste another second. His tongue replaced his finger and ran over my pussy. "Mmm," he moaned against me and a jolt of pleasure shot through me. "You taste so fucking good."

I looked back behind me and saw him on his knees on

the floor. His head was buried between my legs, and it was the headiest sight I had ever seen.

I clamped my eyes closed when he sucked my clit into his mouth, and I pressed my forehead back into the mattress.

I should have been embarrassed by the position I was in front of him, but Olly made me feel comfortable in a way that I didn't understand. Even though my only other sexual experience was traumatic, I didn't question or hesitate with Olly.

I never felt like I needed to.

His fingers pushed into my ass cheeks as he spread me apart to give himself full access, and I moaned as he sucked my clit into his mouth again before rolling his tongue from the front to the back of my pussy.

"This is mine." His words vibrated against my pussy because he didn't stop ravaging me for even a second, and my legs began to tremble.

"Of course it is." I could barely manage to get the words out.

"Has anyone else touched you?" His mouth moved away from me but was replaced by his hand only a second later. He slid a finger in and out of me slowly as he talked. "Has anyone made you come like I do?"

I shook my head against the bed, but that wasn't good enough for him.

"Tell me."

"No. There's no one else." Of course, there was no one else. I couldn't imagine letting anyone else touch me other than him. I wasn't sure that I would ever be able to.

"Thank fuck." His hand moved faster and faster, and he curled his fingers inside me. My knees began to buckle beneath me as he hit a spot inside of me that I had never been able to do on my own, but Olly caught me with his other hand on my hip. "You are my fucking weakness, Frankie. I'm not strong enough to walk away from you."

"I don't want you to be." I pushed back against his hand. "I..." It was on the tip of my tongue to tell him that I just wanted him, but I knew I couldn't have him. Pleasure racked through my body, but I knew that it was temporary. After this ended and my orgasm calmed, I would be walking away from him again.

Olly's tongue joined his hand, and he tasted my entrance as he swirled it around his finger. The sensation was too much, and I felt like I was going to come. I was so lost in the feeling that was racing through me that I barely noticed as he moved.

His lips pressed a gentle kiss against my ass cheek before his teeth grazed over the spot. His other hand replaced where his mouth had just been, and I tensed as he used it to spread me apart again.

"What are you doing?"

"Taking every inch of what's mine." Then his thumb pushed against my tight little hole, and I felt like I was going to die.

I didn't know what to do or say, and I had no idea if I was supposed to like it. But as he began to really move against me, I knew that I didn't want him to stop.

"Oh my God, Olly." My hands tightened in the sheets, and I tried to breathe through the pleasure that was consuming me.

"I know, baby." He didn't stop. He slid his hand from my pussy and spread the moisture over my bud. "You are so fucking beautiful." He continued working me with his hand as his mouth went back to my pussy, and I couldn't escape him even if I wanted to. "Let go," he murmured against me. "I want to feel you come on my face."

He sucked my clit into his mouth as his thumb pressed harder, and my orgasm ripped through my body. I screamed into his mattress, but he didn't stop. He worked me with his mouth until I was gasping for breath, then he reached beneath me and flipped me over onto my back.

"I need to be inside you." He was already pushing his pants down his hips, and I watched in wonder at how breathtaking he was. No amount of time apart could make me forget, but there was something about being away from him for so long that made me crave everything about him even more now.

Olly wrapped his hand around the backside of my knee before tugging me toward the end of his bed. He was so hard, and I couldn't stop the tremor that ran through me as he pushed his cock through my wetness.

He was watching what he was doing, but as he started to push inside me, his gaze met mine. His stare was so intense that I thought it might break me.

He pushed inside me slowly as his fingers dug into my thighs. There was such a harsh contrast between his hands and the way he was looking at me. I adjusted to the size of him as he leaned over me and pushed my hair out of my face.

"You feel so perfect." He moved inside me slowly, and his fingers ran down the side of my face. "So fucking perfect."

He ran his mouth over my lips before moving along my jaw. His mouth followed the pace of his hips, and they were both driving me crazy. I needed him to move faster, harder. I needed him to do anything that didn't make me feel like I was drowning in thoughts of how badly I needed him.

"You are mine," he growled against my neck before grazing the sensitive skin with his teeth.

My hips surged forward to meet his. "Please, Olly."

He lifted my thigh around his hip as he moved me farther up the bed and sat back on his heels. He stared down at me as he moved, still so damn focused and slow. He was savoring this, taking his time with my body, and I wasn't sure that I could handle it.

His hand pressed against my neck, the edge of pain in his touch making my hips move faster against his, before he slowly ran it down my body. His touch was a whisper of contact, and if I wasn't seeing him directly in front of me, I would have thought him a dream.

He caressed his hand from one hip to the other before he trailed it down to my pussy, then everything changed. He slapped his hand down against my clit, and I shot off the bed as a surge of pleasure shot through my body.

He caught me against him with one hand as his other remained on my pussy. He lifted me until we were chest to chest, and I kissed him desperately as he began rubbing rough, quick circles against my clit.

I wrapped my legs around his body and began to move against him. He felt so deep in this position, and I wasn't sure if I had ever felt so full before. I could feel him everywhere. There wasn't an inch of me that wasn't mesmerized by him.

My hands tangled in his hair, and I tugged hard on the strands until he was forced to look up at me. I watched him, the dark brown of his eyes almost black with lust, and I searched for something that I had no business looking for.

"What do you want, Frankie?" he asked as he still moved

inside me. He knew that I was searching for more too. He knew that this would never be enough.

"I don't know." I shook my head, and he slammed inside me.

I moaned and my eyes threatened to close from the pleasure. "Yes. You do." He growled and fucked me even harder. "Do you want me to make you promises that I have no idea I can keep?"

The hopeless look in his eyes made my chest ache. I had no idea what I was looking for or what the hell I was asking. But I knew that I was going to wake up tomorrow and none of this was going to feel right. Because I wanted to demand that he put me first.

I tried to shut it out. To not think about anything outside of this moment, but his next words made that impossible.

"I love you, Frankie."

He pinched my clit between his fingers as he slammed into me and his words echoed through my body. I cried out as the strongest orgasm of my life rushed through me, and he held on to me for dear life.

I could barely catch my breath from him binding me against him in his arms, and I clawed at his neck in an attempt to gain control from where I was spiraling.

Olly groaned against my chest and slammed into me over and over. He tensed under my touch as his body tightened, and I felt him come inside me while my pussy pulsed around him.

Neither one of us said anything or moved for a long time. We just sat there with me in his arms and me holding on to him as if I was scared to let go.

And I knew that was the truth.

I was worried that if I let him go for even a second, he

would slip through my fingers as if he was never meant to be there.

After what felt like forever, Olly laid me back against one of his pillows before climbing off the bed and grabbing a towel from his dresser. We didn't speak as he used it to gently clean me up or as he turned off the light and climbed into the bed beside me.

Panic swarmed my chest when I realized that we hadn't used a condom again, but I had been on birth control for years. Ever since...

He wrapped me in his arms, and I pressed my forehead against his chest. His heart was beating so damn hard, and I knew that mine was doing the same.

He pressed a kiss to the top of my head before his fingers ran over my hair and gently down my back. It felt good. Too good. Like this was exactly where I was meant to be.

It was all I could think about as I started drifting off to sleep, and I knew that I couldn't let this happen. I couldn't be the girl who fell for the lie over and over again. Even if it was just as much my lie as it was his.

Whether Olly loved me or not wasn't important. He was the only person who made me feel alive, but that still wasn't enough.

And it never would be because he wasn't choosing me.

Even though I knew his apology was sincere, words weren't enough. Not anymore.

CHAPTER 17
OLLY

The sun was filtering in through the blinds, and I blinked my eyes open. I was still so damn tired, and my body was exhausted and sore from all the damn preseason workouts we had been doing.

I had played baseball all my life, but I had never worked this hard. My body knew it too.

I rolled over onto my stomach and ran my hand across my bed. Instantly, the smell of her bombarded me, and my eyes shot open.

Fuck. Frankie was here. She was here, and I was such a fucking idiot.

I sat up in my bed and looked around, but there wasn't a single trace of her. If it wasn't for the smell of her on my skin and the deep ache that filled my chest, I wouldn't have believed that she had been there at all.

It wasn't uncommon that I dream of her. It had become my normal, but this was different. She was here, and I had to find her.

I climbed out of my bed and found my sweatpants

thrown on the floor at the end of the bed. I jerked them up my legs before I pulled my bedroom door open.

I could hear Allie and Carson talking in the living room, and I stepped out while running my fingers through my hair.

"Hey." I nodded my head to Carson before looking around my apartment. I didn't see her anywhere. I looked back toward the bathroom, but the door was wide open with the light off. "Have you all seen Frankie?"

They both got quiet, and I brought my gaze back to look at my best friend.

"She left." He winced, and my heart began pounding in my chest.

"What do you mean, she left?"

"Early this morning," Allie finished for him. "She said that she needed to get back home, so she booked an early flight out."

My hands balled into fists as I heard what she said. That didn't make sense. Everything was fine last night when we fell asleep. We had just fucked like two people who were in love with each other. Hell, I told her that I loved her.

And now she was gone?

"Did she say why?" I hesitated for a second, but then the thought of her hopeless-looking face staring down at me last night flashed through my mind. "I have to stop her."

I started back toward my room, but Allie's words stopped me. "She's already gone, and..."

"And what?" I growled at her, and I hated the way she tensed.

"She doesn't want to see you." It was clearly visible how much she hated saying those words out loud.

"What?"

"Just give her time, Olly." Allie shook her head and looked over at Carson.

"Did you sleep with her again?" Carson asked and crossed his arms. "You need to figure out where your fucking head is. You can't make promises to her and to Beck."

"I fucking know that."

"Do you?" He cocked his head to the side.

"Of course, I do." My hands shook at my sides. Frankie had been mine for the summer, and that was over. Everything we had agreed to was over, but it was still breaking me.

Frankie was never truly mine, but losing her was breaking my heart.

And I knew that I couldn't just let it happen.

I couldn't lose her even if that meant losing everything else.

Keep reading for a sneak peek of...

The
TEMPTATION
of
DIRTY SECRETS

CHAPTER 1
FRANKIE

Everyone saw what they wanted to see.

The Clermonts' perfect daughter.

Beck's little sister.

The poor girl that got assaulted.

The one who was so desperate that she was trying to hook up with all of her brother's friends.

I had become an accumulation of these titles they had given me.

They were whispered in the halls at school and stared at me in the faces of everyone I passed.

They all thought they knew exactly who I was, but they didn't have a clue.

I didn't have a fucking clue.

But they had gotten a front-row seat to my heartbreak. They had all seen what Lucas had done to me on the screens of their phones, and they all still gossiped about the way I had told Olly I loved him at that party and how he could barely look me in the eye.

And the assumptions they were making were starting to

eat at me. With every passing second, they became more real.

Olly was my weakness, and he had become my strength.

He had become my safe place and my crutch, and suddenly, I didn't know who I was without him.

I knew the thoughts that were running through my head were irrational, but that didn't make them feel any less real.

I had fallen for Olly. I had given him more of myself than I had ever given anyone, and it wasn't enough.

God, I hated that word.

When would it ever be enough? Was I a good enough daughter? Had I apologized enough to Beck? Had I hated myself enough for what happened with Lucas? Had I tried hard enough to hang on to Olly?

Enough seemed to be the goal that was always in the back of my mind that I could never quite reach.

None of it was enough.

I knew it the moment I opened my eyes while I was still in Olly's arms. Every bit of courage I had been desperately trying to build up fell away as a single thought ran through my head.

I didn't want Olly to love me because he felt like he had to.

He was the best guy I knew, and he would give everything up if that was what I wanted. He had broken my heart, but he would do whatever it took to fix it if I let him.

But that would never be enough for him or for me.

And that was so unhealthy. Everything about us had been from the beginning. I was his secret, he was my obsession, and even though he had been such an integral part in helping me heal, what we had become was toxic for both of us.

It didn't matter that he had already broken my heart when he walked away. Me coming back, me coming here to his place, it had done nothing but fuel his need to protect me.

But I didn't need him to protect me anymore. Not any of them.

I felt trapped by the idea of him constantly feeling the need to save me. I had to learn to save myself.

CHAPTER 2
OLLY

I felt like I was going out of my mind.

It had been less than a week since Frankie left my apartment without a word. A week of texts and calls, and I couldn't take it anymore.

The phone rang over and over as I paced around our small kitchen.

It went to Frankie's voice mail, but I immediately called back.

I was preparing myself for her not to answer again. My hands shook as I thought about what I was going to do. If she wouldn't answer me, then I had no choice but to call Beck.

I had to know that she was okay.

"Hello." Her voice was soft, and she sounded so tired.

"Frankie." I breathed her name with relief. God, I hadn't realized just how bad it was fucking me up that she was refusing to talk to me.

It was destroying me that she left after everything.

"What do you need, Olly? I'm about to walk into English."

Fuck. She was at school. I hadn't even thought about that. I just knew that I couldn't take her ignoring me anymore.

"I just want to talk to you." I ran my fingers over the counter. "I need to apologize."

"There is nothing for you to apologize for. We had our summer, we hurt each other, and now it is time for us to move on."

I shook my head because she was wrong. I had been so fucking wrong.

"You know that's a lie."

She laughed bitterly before she said the next words. "What I know is that I can't do this anymore, Olly. I can't keep allowing someone to have this much power over me. I'm not going to hand over the power for you to hurt me again."

Her words hit me in my gut, and I couldn't breathe.

That was the last thing I wanted. I didn't want to hurt her. I fucking hated the fact that I had done so already.

I had known the moment I had given her up for the sake of anyone other than us I had made a mistake. Fuck, I knew it long before that. But seeing it in her eyes staring back at me, I couldn't hide from it anymore.

I was in love with her, and nothing else mattered.

I was an idiot for believing that it ever did.

"What can I do, Frankie? Do you want me to tell Beck that this is what I want? Do you want me to come home?"

"Don't be insane."

I could hear people around her, and I hated that we were having this conversation like this. I wished she had never left. I wished she had fucking talked to me.

"There is nothing to tell Beck, Olly. You're in California, and I'm here. Please don't make this harder than it has to be."

She was pushing me away. I could hear the edge of panic in her voice, and I knew that this was her way of protecting herself.

I fucking hurt her, and it was too much.

Fear punched me in the chest. I tried to think of the right words, the right thing to do that would save us. It was a battle inside myself between what I knew was good for her and what I felt.

But I knew with certainty that I loved Frankie Clermont. I loved her and she loved me too, but I broke her.

"Just tell me what to do." I was fucking begging her, but I knew that I would do whatever she told me to do. I would do whatever it took to make it up to her.

"Just let me move on, Olly. This isn't healthy," she whispered, and I knew that she was right. What we were doing to each other wasn't good for either of us, but it didn't make me want her any less. "I just need to be able to be okay on my own."

I didn't know how to answer her without lying to her. I wanted that for her too, but it was also the last thing I wanted. I couldn't imagine not being a part of her life. I didn't know how not to love her.

"Okay." I nodded my head and clamped my eyes closed. "I'll let you get to class." We were both silent for a long moment. "You'll call me if you need me?"

"Yeah." Her answer was a lie of her own.

I broke her, and I didn't know what to do.

CHAPTER 3
FRANKIE

One Year Later

I pushed through the crowd of people and made my way up to the bar. I smiled as I caught the attention of my favorite bartender, and he grinned while tossing his towel onto his shoulder.

"What can I do for you, Frankie?"

"Tequila on the rocks with a squeeze of lime."

He laid his elbows against the bar and leaned forward until his face was close to mine. Only a few inches separated us. "Did you notice how packed we are tonight?"

"I did." I nodded and looked to my right where some guy was laughing obnoxiously. "That's what took me so long to get up here. I didn't think I was ever going to make it through the crowd."

"Did you stop and think maybe Greg isn't going to serve me tonight since there are so many people around, and I'm barely a day over nineteen?" He cocked his eyebrow, and I could feel people around us watching us. Not because they were interested, but because they wanted him to hurry and serve them a drink.

"Nope." I shook my head and matched his position. "I'm pretty sure it's impossible for you to tell me no."

He only hesitated for a second before his lips lifted on the side in a cocky smile. "That's the truth. I couldn't tell you no if I wanted to." He chuckled as I handed him a twenty-dollar bill. He grabbed a glass, filled it with ice and a generous amount of tequila before sliding me my drink. His gaze trailed over my face before they stopped on my lips.

"You forgot my lime."

"I didn't forget." He reached for a lime and ran it over the rim of my glass before dropping it inside. "I just wanted to look at you for a few more seconds before you disappeared."

Heat bloomed in my chest, and I knew he could see the blush crossing my face. If I hadn't been thinking about how I had kissed him outside of the bar the week before, I definitely was now.

I shouldn't have done it. It was one of those don't shit where you eat kind of scenarios since this had become my favorite place to drink, but I had one too many tequilas and his face was just a touch too handsome.

"You're too good to me, Greg." I smiled but tried to hide the anxiety that was creeping in. I wasn't interested in kissing him again. I wasn't interested in doing anything with him other than being his friend.

"Be safe." He nodded toward the crowd, and I saluted him before giving him a wink. He was always trying to watch over me, to make sure I was okay, and I should have been flattered by the fact. But I wasn't.

Because it reminded me too much of him, and I hated anything that reminded me of him.

I smiled and turned around with my drink in my hand. I was about to walk away when I bumped into someone and knocked my drink between our chests.

"Oh my God. I'm so sorry." I stumbled over my words as I fumbled for napkins off the bar behind me and tried to blot at the liquid that was now coating his shirt.

"It's okay." He chuckled and took one of the napkins from my hand. "I didn't get much on me."

I looked up just as he took the napkin and wiped it across my own shirt. The tequila was soaking through my white tank top and the work he was doing wasn't going to make one bit of difference.

But I didn't stop him.

I couldn't have if I wanted to because I was too busy noticing how his eyes were the same color as my favorite shade of the ocean, and how his white button-up molded to his chest.

"I didn't even see you standing there. I'm so sorry. This place is so crowded tonight." I straightened out my shirt that was now clinging to my chest as he tossed the soiled napkins on the counter.

"It's not a big deal," he reassured me as he smiled. "What were you drinking? I'll get you another."

"You don't have to do that." I shook my head, but he was moving the few steps toward the bar and lifting his hand in the air.

"It's the least I can do." The way he was looking at me forced me to look away. He looked at me like he saw something more than what I was. Something that could be more than this moment.

He was a perfect stranger, but he was looking at me like I was the best thing he had seen all night.

"Why's that?"

"Well, you say you didn't see me, but I haven't been able to take my eyes off you." His gaze skimmed over my face. "I was coming over here to talk to you and caused you to spill your drink."

I looked back at him and searched his face as he smiled. He was handsome, there was no denying that, but my stomach didn't flutter as he spoke. If anything, listening to what he was saying did nothing but make me crave that feeling. A feeling I had been missing for far longer than I liked to admit. "Tequila on the rocks with lime."

"Okay." There was a low rumble in his voice, and the way he smiled was like he knew something that I didn't. He thought that my drink order was a sign that I was interested in him, but I wasn't. I hadn't been interested in anyone since him.

He nodded toward Greg and caught his attention, and he stopped in front of him before his gaze slid to me. "Can I get a tequila on the rocks?"

"With lime," Greg finished for him before he could.

"Exactly." He chuckled and turned to look back at me. "What's your name?"

"Frankie." I tucked my hair behind my ear before sliding my hands into my back pockets. "You?"

"Ben."

"It's nice to meet you." I felt awkward standing there waiting for my drink, and if I wasn't in desperate need of tequila, I probably would have already bounced.

"You too. You go to the university?"

"Yeah." I nodded and watched as Greg made my drink. "Business major."

"Me too." He chuckled and rapped his knuckles against the bar. "I can't believe I've never seen you before."

"Maybe you have and just didn't realize." I shrugged. I saw hundreds of people at this damn school every day, and I could barely remember any of their faces.

"No. Trust me. I would remember."

My skin heated, and I opened my mouth to respond just as Greg slid my drink in front of Ben and looked at me. "You okay?"

"Yeah." I flushed with embarrassment as I nodded.

"Make sure you come to see me before you leave."

Ben looked back and forth between us, but I tried not to look at either of them.

"I will." I nodded again and took a long drink of my tequila.

It burned my throat with a deliciousness that I craved.

I stepped away from the bar, and Ben followed me.

"You got a thing with the bartender?"

His question annoyed me, but I tried to let it roll off my back. "I don't have a thing with anyone."

I pushed through the crowd, and he was at my back the whole time. I should have been flattered by his interest in me, but I couldn't force myself to be.

I made it to the table where my friends were sitting and took my empty seat. Ben grabbed a chair from the table next to us and pulled it up next to me.

Dawn raised her eyebrows at me in question as she watched him settle in beside me, and I shrugged my shoulders and tried to stop myself from rolling my eyes.

I met Dawn on the day we moved into our apartment

together, and we hit it off instantly. She was my go-to girl when it came to escaping my own thoughts and losing ourselves out at the bar.

I smiled over at Ben who was watching me and pulled my phone out of my pocket. The music was blaring in the bar, so I didn't feel the overwhelming need to make small talk, but I still felt awkward.

There was a text from Josie on my phone, and I winced as I read it.

Josie: What are you doing tonight? I feel like we've barely talked all week.

That was because we hadn't. The university was only about a twenty-minute drive back to my parents' house, and even though I still spent most of my time there, sometimes it became overwhelming.

Everything reminded me of Olly, and when I heard Beck talk about him, I had to smile and pretend like he didn't matter to me. I had to act like I hadn't spent the entire last year trying to force myself to think about anything other than him.

I had barely seen him over the past year, but it didn't matter. Every time I did, it was like no time had passed. He was still the boy I was in love with, and I was still the girl who couldn't have him.

I was the girl who pushed him away.

And now he was in love with someone else.

"Do you come here a lot?"

"What?" I looked up from my phone to Ben, and I almost forgot he was sitting there.

"This bar." He motioned around us. "Do you come here a lot?"

"Oh. Yeah." I nodded. "It's the best place to get tequila when you're only nineteen."

He laughed and rubbed his hand over the smattering of hair on his jaw. That one simple move reminded me of Olly, and a deep ache pressed against my chest.

"I guess you have a good point there. What year are you?"

"Freshman. You?" I nodded in his direction. He was definitely older than me, but he wasn't too much older.

"Senior."

"Oh, Frankie!" Dawn leaned forward and rubbed her hands together playfully. "It looks like you have caught yourself a daddy."

Ben blanched and stuttered over his next words. "I don't have any kids."

I rolled my eyes as Dawn laughed, and leaned closer to him so he could hear me. "That's not what she means. She's calling you a daddy because you're older."

"Oh." He wrinkled his brow, and honestly, I could tell he was going to be a ball of fun.

"I'm taking it you've never dated a younger girl before." I didn't know why I said that. He obviously wasn't dating me, and I had no plans to change that. Guys like Ben reminded me too much of the guys in Clermont Bay, the guys I was forced to spend my last year of high school with while I was miserable, and I had no interest in spending even more time with them.

It didn't matter how handsome he was.

Nothing seemed to matter because every time I thought I could move past Olly, I couldn't. I just compared every single move they made, everything about them, to him.

And it wasn't fucking fair.

"No." He shook his head. "This would be a first for me."

"Whoa, whoa, whoa." I lifted my glass of tequila and downed the rest of the clear liquid. "No one said there was a this."

He winced, and I instantly felt bad. "That's not what I meant. I wasn't saying…"

"I'm just busting your balls." I smiled and set down my glass. "So, Business Major Ben, are you local, or did you move here for college?"

"I moved here." He pressed his elbows into his knees and leaned forward. "I'm originally from Texas."

"I thought I heard a little twang in there." I tapped my ear, and he laughed.

"I do everything in my power to get rid of that twang and everything I left in Texas." He smiled softly, but it was hiding something beneath that I couldn't quite place.

It made me more interested in him than I had been in anyone in a long time.

"What about you? You a local girl?"

"I am." I nodded and gripped the sides of my seat. "My parents live a few miles north of here."

"They on the coast?"

"Yeah." I nodded.

"That's awesome." His gaze ran over my face. "I love the ocean. The sounds, the smell."

I nodded as I could practically imagine what he was saying. "Me too. It's my favorite place in the world."

"I wouldn't have left here either."

I couldn't tell him that the reason I didn't leave was that I had been hoping and praying that my staying would mean that Olly would eventually come back. Even though I knew

Clermont Bay was the last place he wanted to be, deep down I was holding out hope that he would come back for me.

I was the one who had pushed him away. I told him that this thing between us couldn't work, and I knew that was the truth. But I also knew that deep down, I still craved every part of him.

And that was fucking pathetic.

I didn't have time to constantly think about Olly.

Beck had been working hard with my father over the last year, and he had taken so much of my father's responsibilities on that I didn't have to shoulder any of them.

And I knew Beck did that for me. He did that because he wanted me to go to college and live the dream, as he quoted to me often. But I always used my family as an excuse for why I stayed.

My parents were both doing well; my dad was smiling more now that he had Beck in the position to help him, and I liked to pretend that they needed me more than they did.

Because if they needed me, then I wasn't wasting my life by staying here. If they needed me, then I wasn't as big of a fool as I truly knew I was.

Because I had pushed Olly away, and even though nothing really was, I felt like I was falling apart.

I pushed Olly away because I knew he wasn't good for me, but I desperately wanted him to be.

"I'm actually going home this weekend for this little get-together at my parents' house." *What the hell are you doing, Frankie?* "Do you want to come with me?"

He grinned, deep and genuine, and I wished it affected me more than it did. "A moment ago you were giving me shit over there not being a this" —he motioned his hand back and forth between us— "and now you want to take me home to meet the parents?"

I winced because he was right, but there was no going back now. "My parents won't actually be there. But you will meet my older brother, which is actually worse. Take it or leave it."

"Take it." He watched me and searched my eyes. "I'm definitely going to take it."

CHAPTER 4
OLLY

"This is so good, Carson." Jordan looked up at my friend and smiled before glancing back at me. "Thank you for cooking."

"You're welcome." He smiled back at her even though he didn't like her. I would even dare to say that he hated her even though he would never admit it.

He had hated her from the moment he met her.

"What time do we have to be at workouts?" I avoided his gaze and took the last bite off my plate.

"Thirty minutes." He dropped his dishes into the sink, then looked back over at me. "Be ready in ten."

"I'll be ready." I turned back to Jordan and pushed some of her soft brown hair over her shoulder. She smiled up at me like she always did, like I was the best thing that ever happened to her, and guilt clawed at my chest.

Because even though I really liked Jordan, she would never be Frankie.

And that was so fucked up.

I was more than aware of that fact. It had been a year

since Frankie and I were last together. Over a year since she ran out of my apartment like she couldn't get away from me fast enough, but I still couldn't get her out of my head.

I couldn't make my chest quit aching when I thought about her every time I kissed Jordan. I was doing everything in my power to move on from her, but it didn't seem to matter.

Everything reminded me of her. Everything Jordan did, I compared to her.

It didn't matter that I was using Jordan to drown out my need for Frankie. It wasn't intentional, or at least it hadn't been in the beginning, but I slipped into that vice so easily.

Frankie was the person I never stopped looking for.

I didn't know how to move past it, past her, and part of me knew that I didn't want to. Not really. I wanted to cling to the feeling that she gave me. A feeling that I hadn't been able to find anywhere else.

"You want me to walk you out to your car?"

"No. I'll be fine." She shook her head just as Carson left the room. "I'd rather spend a few minutes alone before I go."

"I know, but I can't be late." My chest tightened even harder. It wasn't a lie, but it also wasn't the whole truth. But I couldn't tell her that I had seen a post Frankie made on Instagram earlier, and now even my normal tricks to clear my mind of her weren't working. "Coach will have my ass."

"I know." She nodded, but I could see the hurt in her eyes. She knew that something was off with me. Jordan and I had been dating for less than six months, but Frankie wasn't something we talked about anymore. I had told her about Frankie once on a drunken night when I was pushing her away, but she's never brought her up since. "I'll see you later?"

"Yeah." I leaned forward and pressed my lips to her forehead. "I'll text you as soon as I get back."

She wrapped her hands around my neck, pulling me down until my lips met hers, and she kissed me like she was scared it wouldn't happen again. It always felt like that, like I was kissing her goodbye.

I pulled away from her when it was clear that she wasn't going to, and she looked up at me with such sad eyes. That was something that she and Frankie had in common. They were both so fucking expressive with one simple look.

But while Jordan's filled me with guilt, a look from Frankie could cut me to my core.

Jordan walked out the door, and I ran my fingers through my hair before I stood. It took me no time to get my gear on even though my head still felt like it was clouded by a million different thoughts. I had no interest in going to workouts.

Fuck. I didn't want to do anything, but pick up my phone and try to call Frankie.

My hand shook around my phone as I stared down at her name, and it took everything inside of me not to call her. I clicked it off before sliding it into my shorts and walking out of my room.

Carson and Garrett were waiting on me in the living room when I walked out, and I tried to push away all thoughts of her as I faced my friends.

"What's up, fucker?" Garrett tossed his Gatorade bottle from one hand to the next. Garrett was on our team, and at our apartment more than not. Most of the time it felt like he lived here.

"Nothing."

"Told you." Carson grabbed his bag and headed toward the door without another word.

"You told him what?" I followed behind him, grabbing my bag along the way. Neither one of them answered me until we had climbed into Garrett's truck, and he pulled out of the parking lot.

"Carson just said that you were moping around a bit today."

"Correction." Carson held up his finger. "I told him that you were being a moody bitch."

I rolled my eyes at both of them and pulled my phone back out of my pocket. "I am not being moody. I have a fucking headache."

"You sure do." Carson nodded, and it grated on my nerves.

"Just say whatever it is you want to say, Carson. I'm seriously not in the mood." I clicked on Instagram and scrolled through my feed absentmindedly.

"Why are you still doing this bullshit with Jordan when you're still not over Frankie?"

"Considering I've barely talked to or seen Frankie in the last year, I'd say I'm fucking over her." It was a lie that neither one of us believed.

"Am I going to meet this legendary Frankie when we go to Clermont Bay this weekend?"

"Absolutely."

"Probably not," Carson and I answered at the exact same time.

Carson turned in his seat to get a better look at me. "Do you honestly think we're going to go back, and you're not going to see her?"

I shrugged my shoulders because that was exactly what I

thought. "She's away for college, and from what Josie tells me, partying all the time. I highly doubt she'll be in Clermont Bay." The thought alone ate at me. I was always so damn worried about her, and I wasn't there. I wasn't there, and she was moving on.

"You're delusional." He searched my face, and I knew he was looking for whatever it was I wasn't telling him. But he wouldn't find it. I had become an expert in locking away my feelings for Frankie. At least from others.

Most days I felt like I was dying on the inside without her, but I could hide it. I had to hide it.

"Well." I shrugged again. "We'll either see her or we won't."

"It doesn't matter to you either way." I couldn't tell if it was a statement or a question.

"It doesn't."

"Uh-huh," he said that so sarcastically. "And I bet that when you see her, you won't be affected by her in the least."

"Correct." I stared him down and tried to get him to drop it. I wasn't in the mood to talk about Frankie. I wasn't strong enough.

"And I bet you won't be bothered at all by the fact that she apparently has a boyfriend now?"

His words hit me directly in my chest, and I felt like I couldn't breathe. Thoughts of her with someone else flashed through my mind and hit me like a train as my hands began to shake at my sides. I knew that wasn't fair. I was with Jordan. I had been with Jordan, and I couldn't expect Frankie to just be alone.

I didn't expect her to, but fuck, I don't know. I also didn't like to think about her being with anyone else. I had avoided that thought like the fucking plague.

In my head, Frankie was still mine. It didn't matter that I hadn't talked to her in what felt like forever, and it had been months since I smelled the soft coconut scent of her skin.

Hell, the last time I saw her, she practically acted like she didn't know me at all. But she did. She knew me better than anyone else.

And she still felt like mine.

"Shit. I shouldn't have said anything."

I blinked up at Carson because I had honestly forgotten that he was even there. "No. It's fine." I could barely manage to get the words out.

"It's not fine." He shook his head. "Nothing about this whole damn thing is fine. You should go home and demand that Frankie talk to you."

Demand she talk to me. I wished it were that easy. If I could simply demand that she talk to me, then I wouldn't be here right now. Because I had tried. Over and over, and Frankie didn't want to talk to me.

She had made that perfectly clear through the unanswered calls and one-word text message replies.

I wished that I could just hold her face in my hands and demand that she look at me and actually see me for the first time in what felt like forever.

I wanted her to see and hear how badly I missed her.

I couldn't grasp all the thoughts that were flashing through my head. Was she even the same Frankie that I knew? Had she changed so much that maybe she didn't think about me the way I still thought about her?

Maybe that was a good thing.

Frankie deserved to move on. Even if I couldn't. She deserved to be happy in whatever way she could.

She had told me so herself.

She was trying to move on, and I had to let her.

But that didn't mean that it still hadn't felt like a betrayal. Every time I touched Jordan, the betrayal I felt ate at me a little more and more.

Frankie wasn't even talking to me anymore, and I still felt like I was betraying her every day. But she was leaving me with no choice but to force myself to move on from her.

I fucked up when I hurt her. I hurt her, and did nothing but push her away.

We had been each other's secrets, and she deserved to be my truth. She always had.

"What would you like me to say to her?" I rubbed my hand over the back of my neck as we pulled into the school parking lot. I spotted half our team climbing out of their cars, and this was the last damn place I wanted to be. "Nothing is different between us. There isn't a damn thing for either one of us to say."

"Then you're a bigger idiot than I thought."

CHAPTER 5
FRANKIE

I felt like I had just fallen asleep when my phone rang, but as I felt around for the blaring thing, I noticed the time on my clock.

Two-oh-five in the morning.

I blinked past the brightness of my screen and hit Answer before pressing my phone to my ear.

"Hello." I let my eyes fall back closed, and I was almost back asleep when I heard his voice come through the phone.

"Fuck. Are you asleep?"

"Olly?" I knew it was him, but it had been so damn long since I talked to him that I felt a bit shocked at hearing his voice.

"Yeah." He chuckled softly. "I'm sorry. I didn't mean to wake you."

My heart hammered in my chest, and every trace of the heaviness that threatened to pull me back to sleep fell away in an instant.

"No. It's okay." I sat up in bed and pulled my knees against my chest. "I was just shocked to hear your voice."

He was quiet for another moment. "I know. I probably shouldn't have called."

"I'm glad you did," I hurried to reassure him before he could get off the phone. I felt like I had been ignoring him for so long that I couldn't remember why this wasn't a good idea.

One small whisper of his voice was pure temptation. It was like a dirty secret in the dead of the night, and no one could see us. No one was here to tell me that still wanting him was wrong.

And me wanting him was the only real truth that I knew. Everything else felt like I was faltering, pretending, guessing my way through life, but he had never felt like that. Even when I knew we weren't good for each other, he was real.

"I'm glad you finally answered." He was quiet for a long moment, and I didn't reply because, what was there to say? I couldn't tell him that wasn't the truth when we both knew damn well that it was. "Carson and I are coming to town this weekend. Are you going to be there, or will you be at school?"

I bit down on my bottom lip as I thought about my stupid fucking plan to invite Ben along for the trip. It had felt like a good idea at the time, but I was regretting it now.

"Yeah. I'll be there." I nodded even though he couldn't see it, and ran my hand over my sheets. "Josie would kill me if I missed Beck's birthday party."

"Same." He chuckled softly, and my thighs tightened at the sound. "Apparently being across the country wasn't a good enough excuse to miss it."

"Did you need an excuse to miss it?" I knew I shouldn't have asked the question because I really didn't want to know his answer.

"I don't know." There was fumbling on his end of the line, and I tried to imagine what he was doing. "I honestly didn't think you'd want to see me there. Not after the last time..."

When I had done everything in my power to pretend like he wasn't important to me.

"You're still my friend, Olly." Saying his name out loud felt forbidden on my tongue. I hadn't said it in so long because I knew what those two damn syllables could do to me.

"Am I? We don't feel much like friends anymore."

I didn't know how to answer him because he was right. We didn't feel like friends. It was as if suddenly, we were strangers again.

I was still in love with a boy who had become a stranger to me, and I didn't know how to stop.

"You'll always be my friend, Olly. Things have just been..." I hesitated because I didn't want to give too much of myself away. If I finished that sentence, if I told him how hard things had been for me when I knew he had moved on, I would be handing things over to him that I promised I never would again.

"Fucking miserable." He huffed as my chest ached, and I could imagine him running his fingers through his hair as he overthought everything he was saying. "I've been fucking miserable without you."

I slammed my eyes closed and tried to block out his words. I tried not to let them have the kind of effect on me that I already knew they would have.

"I can't do this."

"Can't do what?" He sounded so desperate. "All we're doing is having a conversation."

"No." I shook my head and pulled my sheet against my chest. "What we're doing is hurting each other."

Because he had hurt me. Completely and irrevocably, and I couldn't give him that power again. I was so tired of letting others have power over me.

"You're the one who walked out on me." His voice was so somber, and I would have felt bad if anger didn't flush every surface of my skin.

"And you're the one who made a promise that you would have nothing to do with me again."

"I broke that promise, didn't I?"

"You seem to break a lot of promises." That was a low blow, and I knew it. I knew what Olly and I had been getting into when we started.

"I didn't make you any promises, Frankie. We knew we couldn't have any promises between us."

"Just secrets," I whispered, and I hated how battered I felt. It didn't matter how much time had passed between us, how long it had been since I heard his voice, it all came flooding back to me with no effort. "Do you make promises to your girlfriend?" I pushed the anger forward and tried with everything I had to get it to overtake the heartbreak. "Is she asleep beside you right now or are you hiding me again?"

He didn't answer at first, and for a long moment, I didn't think he was going to.

"I heard that you've got yourself a boyfriend."

Ben wasn't my boyfriend, not even close, but there was no way in hell I was going to let Olly know that. Especially when I could hear the jealousy in his voice. "Is that an issue?"

"Of course, it's a fucking issue," he growled, and I pushed my thighs together at the sound.

"Is that why you're calling me? You're upset that I'm with someone else?"

"Don't do that, Frankie." I could hear his irritation dripping from his voice. "You know that I have tried to call you over and over, and you haven't wanted anything to do with me. I just..."

I pushed the guilt away and clung to my anger. "You what? You get to go fuck whoever you want. You get to fuck that girl that you were supposedly just friends with when I came to visit you, but I'm not supposed to do the same? I hate to tell you this, Olly, but you don't have to hear about a guy being my boyfriend for me to be fucking him."

It was a lie. A huge fucking lie.

Because despite how hard I was trying to act, I hadn't gotten over Olly in any way. Not emotionally and not physically. He was fucking his girlfriend like I had never mattered at all, and I could barely bring myself to touch another man.

"Don't say shit like that, Frankie. I don't want to think about you with anyone else." I could hear the anger in his voice, and I was grateful. Let him be angry.

"And you think I do? Do you really think I want to be reminded of how easily you moved on all the time?"

"I haven't moved on. I waited for you, and you're the one who told me you didn't want this. You're the one who told me to find someone else."

"And clearly you have. You're dating someone else, Olly. You've been dating her."

"And every time I close my eyes and touch her, I think about you."

I couldn't breathe as he spoke. His words were faint and reckless, and I knew that I shouldn't have drank them down as if it was the most honest thing I had ever heard.

"Olly."

"It's true." There was rustling on his end of the phone, and I pressed my back against my pillows as I tried to calm my racing heart.

"I haven't talked to you in forever, and now you're calling me to tell me that... that you..."

"That I still imagine your face when my cock is in my hand. That I can't get off without thinking about the way you smell, the way you taste. That you fucked me up so badly that no one else compares to you."

I swallowed hard and tried to keep the emotion and lust from filling my voice. "If Jordan isn't doing it for you, you can always find someone else that's better in bed."

"It doesn't have a fucking thing to do with that and you know it."

I bit down on my bottom lip as he spoke.

"Jordan doesn't do it for me because I'm not in fucking love with Jordan."

Don't say it. Don't say it.

"I can't love her because I'm still in love with you."

I knew he could hear my harsh breathing through the phone, but I had no way of stopping it. I didn't know what to say. I didn't know how to lie to him and save myself.

"Tell me you don't love me too, and we can hang up right now. Tell me you don't love me, and I'll let you go be happy as you fucking want to with your new boyfriend."

I chewed on the side of my thumb as I tried to gather the courage to lie to him. It was just a few simple words. "I can't."

He took a sharp breath, and I knew he was going to say something that I wouldn't recover from.

"But that doesn't mean anything."

"The fuck it doesn't," he growled. "What do you want me to do, Frankie?"

He was saying the things that I had wanted to hear for so long, but it still wasn't enough. Not after everything. "There's nothing for you to do. You are in California, and you have a girlfriend. We are bad for each other, Olly. Nothing is going to happen between us."

"We both know that is a lie."

"I don't."

"Yes. You do." Every word was perfectly clear. "Can I FaceTime you? I need to see you."

My heart rate spiked, and I ran my fingers through my hair. "That's not a good idea."

He didn't care about my answer. My phone started beeping, notifying me that he was FaceTiming me, and my finger shook as it hovered over the Answer button. I knew that I shouldn't. If I were smart, I would have hung up the damn phone and gone right back to sleep.

But I was never smart when it came to Olly.

That was the problem.

I pressed Answer, and a heaviness instantly hit my chest as soon as his face came into view. He was laying in his bed, just like me, and his gaze ran over every part of me that he could see through the phone.

I turned on my side with my head resting on my pillow. "If I had known you were going to call me in the middle of the night, I would have dressed better for bed."

He shook his head softly. "You're fucking gorgeous."

"Olly, what are we doing?"

His hair was disheveled and falling in his face, and I knew he had probably been running his fingers through it. It made my own hand itch to do the same.

"I just want to look at you." His tongue ran over his bottom lip. "The last time I was in town you barely let me catch a glance of you before you disappeared."

"The last time you were in town, I couldn't handle seeing you."

His gaze was on fire as he stared back at me. It didn't matter that it was dark on both of our ends, I didn't need light to see the way he was looking at me. I would have been able to feel it with my eyes closed.

"Are you going to ignore me this weekend?"

"That depends?"

"On what?"

"Are you bringing your girlfriend in town with you?"

He winced as I asked the question, but we couldn't pretend like him being with someone else wasn't the truth. He may have been able to forget about her, but I couldn't.

I thought about her every single day.

"I'm not."

A little bit of the tightness in my chest lifted at his words. I saw her on social media, but I didn't think I could handle actually seeing her again. I didn't think my heart would survive really watching him with somebody else.

"Okay." I blinked up at him.

"But you are bringing your boyfriend?" I saw the way his neck tightened and his jaw tensed.

"I am." Even if Ben didn't mean shit to me, I needed him as a buffer. I needed anything that would help protect me from falling right back into Olly.

Because I knew that I would. It would take absolutely no effort for me to forget why he was bad for me. Even talking to him now, it was hard to remember.

"Are you in love with him?"

My gaze snapped back to meet Olly's. "Why would you ask me that?"

"Because I need to know." He adjusted the pillow behind his head roughly. "It drives me crazy to even think about."

"We just started seeing each other, Olly. It's not that serious, and that's not fair."

"Does he make you come like I used to?"

My heart rate spiked as I stared at him. "I'm not going to answer that."

"Because we both already know the truth." He ran his gaze over me, and it didn't matter that he was thousands of miles away. Every inch that his gaze fell on fueled something inside me. "He'll never be able to make you feel like I do."

"You don't make me feel anything anymore, Olly," I answered him and let him hear every bit of anger in my voice.

"We can change that." He ran his fingers through his hair. "It's just you and me here. We can feel whatever we want to feel."

I clamped my thighs together and tried to not let him see how badly his words affected me. "Olly."

"Show me, Frankie." He was watching me so intently. "Show me how you touch yourself."

"This is wrong. We shouldn't be doing this." My hand slid down my belly even as I said the words. I knew I would regret this. It was a mistake, but I felt like a junkie as he spoke. I had been dying for a hit of him.

"Stop worrying about what you should be doing and do what feels right."

I watched him as he adjusted himself in his bed, and I knew that he was touching himself by the way the look on his face shifted. "This feels right. Doesn't it?"

I slid my fingers into my panties, and I was so wet. He wasn't even here, and I was still so wet for him. I ran my finger over my clit and whimpered when a shot of pleasure coursed through me.

"That's it, baby." His voice was so rough. "Imagine that your hand is mine. Think about how desperate I'll be when I finally get to touch you. How hard it will be for me to be easy on you."

My fingers circled my clit, and I sped up as his words fueled me on. I hadn't been this turned on in so long. Not since him.

"How wet are you, Frankie? Tell me."

"I'm so wet." I could barely speak as my orgasm started to build.

"Let me see it. Show me your fingers." His arm was pumping faster and faster.

I pulled my fingers from my pussy with a whimper and showed him. You could see how wet they were, even on the phone screen, and his deep groan told me just how much he liked it.

"Taste it. Tell me if it's as sweet as I remember."

I slid my fingers into my mouth as he watched me, and the way he was looking at me made me feel like I couldn't breathe.

"Fuck." His gaze didn't veer from me as he watched every second of me sucking the wetness from my fingers. "Put them back in your pussy. Show me how badly you wish I was there."

I did so immediately. My body begging for release. I sat up in the bed and slid my panties down my legs. Olly didn't say anything as he watched me, and my hands shook as I propped my phone up on a pillow in front of me and spread my thighs.

"Oh, fuck." Olly jerked forward with a deep groan, and I slid my fingers back through my wetness. I spread it around as he watched, and it felt like the strongest aphrodisiac.

I let my fingers slide into me as I caressed my left breast through my t-shirt with my other hand. "I want to see you too."

Olly rustled around for a moment before he fixed his own phone, and his body came into view. I could still see his face, but I also had a perfect view of his shirtless torso and his cock gripped tightly in his hand.

My fingers sped up as I watched him.

"You are so goddamned beautiful, Frankie. I wish I was the one touching you. I wish I could fuck you with my mouth before I slammed my cock inside of you."

He was pumping his hand harder and faster against his cock, and I followed his lead.

"I want to fuck every inch of you. I would fucking remind you exactly who you belong to."

I whimpered as my orgasm built and built, and I knew that I was so damn close to coming.

"Because you do belong to me, Frankie. Your body, your heart, that perfect little pussy. Every fucking bit of you belongs to me."

I was almost there. So damn close.

"Tell me, baby. Tell me who it all belongs to."

"You." My answer was instant because there wasn't a single question. I had belonged to him for as long as I could remember, and I didn't think there was anything I could do to change that.

Deep down, I was starting to question why I ever wanted to.

"That's fucking right, Frankie. Now come on your fingers while I watch. Show me how badly you wish I was there. Imagine you're coming all over my cock while I fuck every bit of that pleasure from your body."

I tightened my hand around my breast and pushed hard against my clit as my orgasm bombarded me. I screamed his name, and I didn't care that my roommate might hear or the people in the apartment next to us. I had needed that release for so damn long, and my fingers alone had never been enough.

Not like this.

"Fuck." Olly groaned loudly and pointed his cock toward his stomach. I watched as his cum squirted out against his skin and covered his belly.

We sat there in silence for a long time. Both of us trying to catch our breaths and neither of us speaking. I didn't know what to say. I didn't know how to act after what we had just done. We were just watching each other and saying so many things that would never be said out loud.

But even with as good as this felt, I knew it was wrong.

"Are you okay?" His voice startled me.

"Yeah." I nodded and pulled my blanket up to my chest to cover me. I wasn't okay. I didn't know how to be okay. "But I need to get some sleep."

"Yeah." He nodded in agreement. "Me too."

Neither of us hung up, though. We just sat there in silence watching each other breathe, and he was the last thing I saw when my eyes fluttered closed, and I drifted off to sleep.

THANK YOU

Thank you so much for reading the beginning of Frankie and Olly's story! Their story continues in The Temptation of Dirty Secrets, and I'm so excited about the conclusion to this series.

I would love for you to join my reader group, Hollywood, so we can connect and talk about all of your The Seduction of Pretty Lies thoughts. This group is the first place to find out about cover reveals, book news, and new releases!

You can also sign up for my newsletter here: Newsletter

Again, thank you for going on this journey with me.

Xo,
Holly Renee
www.authorhollyrenee.com

Before You Go
Please consider leaving an honest review.